Under the Stars

Jody began shouting at the boys. "Hey! Get out of the water! Leave those dolphins alone!" Her heart was pounding. Now she could see that the bigger boy was riding Evie. The other one had Misty backed against the wall of the pool. "You'll hurt them!" she cried, coming closer. "Get away from them!"

"It's only a kid," sneered the older boy. "She can't stop us. . . ."

But as he spoke, Evie suddenly decided she'd had enough. With one flex of her big, powerful body she threw her rider. The boy went splashing into the water with a yell of surprise.

Look out for more titles in this series

Dolphin Diaries ™

Ben M. Baglio

Illustrations by Judith Lawton

UNDER THE STARS

AN
APPLE
PAPERBACK

SCHOLASTIC INC.
New York   Toronto   London   Auckland   Sydney
Mexico City   New Delhi   Hong Kong   Buenos Aires

No part of this publication may be reproduced in whole or in part, or stored in a retrieval system, or transmitted in any form or by any means, electronic, mechanical, photocopying, recording, or otherwise, without written permission of the publisher. For information regarding permission, write to: Working Partners Limited, 1 Albion Place, London W6 0QT United Kingdom.

ISBN 0-439-31950-1

All rights reserved. Published by Scholastic Inc., 555 Broadway, New York, NY 10012, by arrangement with Working Partners Limited. DOLPHIN DIARIES is a trademark of Working Partners Limited. SCHOLASTIC, APPLE PAPERBACKS, and associated logos are trademarks and/or registered trademarks of Scholastic Inc.

22 21 20 19 18 17 16 15   6/0

Printed in the U.S.A.   40
First Scholastic printing, January 2002

Special thanks to Lisa Tuttle

Thanks also to Dr. Horace Dobbs at
International Dolphin Watch for reviewing the
information contained in this book

1

August 18 — late morning, Nassau, Bahamas.
I'm fed up!

We're supposed to be leaving today, but it's nearly noon and we are still tied to the dock while Mom and Dad finish updating our website and sending e-mails. It costs so much to go on-line out at sea that they want to get it all done now. I wouldn't mind going on-line myself, to send an e-mail to Lindsay (even though there's no news), but Brittany insists it's her turn. I sure wish I didn't have to share my computer!

With a sigh, Jody stopped writing. She was perched on the forward deck of *Dolphin Dreamer*, her favorite place for dolphin-watching when they were at sea. She raised her eyes and scanned the harbor. Earlier, she had spotted something that might have been a porpoise, but it had been too far away to identify. She hoped it would come closer.

It was very quiet. Jody looked at the boats tied up on either side. Usually, people were coming and going constantly in the busy marina, but now she didn't see anyone around. There wasn't a breath of wind, and the clouds massed overhead were very dark.

Suddenly, it began to rain. Jody gasped. She felt as if somebody had poured a bucket of water over her head. And it didn't stop.

Jody scrambled to her feet, holding her diary close. All around, the rain hammered on the deck and on her, like a shower turned on full force. She hurried to get inside.

Her parents, Craig and Gina McGrath, were at the table in the main cabin, sharing a computer. They looked up from their work as she came down the hatch.

"Sweetheart, you're soaked!" cried her mother.

"Did you fall overboard?" Her father grinned and raised his eyebrows quizzically.

Jody shook her head, sending droplets of water flying around the table.

"Hey, watch it!" Brittany cried. "Don't get me all wet, too!" She held her hands up, as if Jody were a dog who might come bounding closer.

"Sorry," Jody said with a sigh.

Maddie, the McGraths' assistant, threw her a towel.

Jody caught it gratefully. "Thanks," she said, returning Maddie's amused smile. She carefully dabbed at her diary, relieved to see that the water hadn't harmed it. "You wouldn't believe how hard it's coming down!" she added as she began to rub herself dry.

Brittany looked worried. She turned to her father, the boat's captain, and asked anxiously, "It's not going to be a hurricane, is it?"

Harry Pierce gave his daughter a reassuring look and shook his head. "No, love. I'm on top of the weather reports, don't you worry! It may be hurricane season, but this is just another tropical shower — like the two we had last week. I think it'll all be over in half an hour, and we can set sail then." He turned to look at Craig. "That is, if you're ready to go?"

Jody had the feeling that Harry was as eager to get going as she was!

"I think we're about ready," Craig replied, smiling. "In fact —"

"Wait, we're getting another e-mail," Gina interrupted him. "Maybe it's from my sister!" Then she frowned, disappointed. "No, it's from Matt."

Jody looked across at the computer screen, interested. They had just spent several weeks with Matt Anderson, who ran a long-term project studying the lives of the Atlantic spotted dolphins living around Little Bahama Bank. She had become friends with several of the dolphins during their stay. "Does he say anything about the dolphins?" she asked, going to stand behind her mother.

"Oh, no," Gina groaned.

Jody read the on-screen message:

Alicia Levy says she hasn't heard from you yet. Why not? Don't forget to visit Dolphin Haven! You'll regret it if you miss this one, I promise! Love, Matt.

She frowned, puzzled. "What's Dolphin Haven?" she asked, turning to her father.

"It's another research facility," Craig explained. "Marine mammal vets Alicia and Dan Levy set it up a few years ago, and by all accounts they're doing some amazing work." He made a rueful face. "I kind of promised Matt we'd pay them a visit."

Gina shook her head. "I know. I know you did, honey. But I think we should forget it," she said. "After all, we can't visit every single dolphin researcher in the world. . . ." She looked at Craig.

He nodded thoughtfully.

"Why don't I send a friendly e-mail to Alicia Levy," Gina suggested. "I'll apologize for not visiting in person and invite her to share her work by uploading some info to the Dolphin Universe website."

Craig nodded. "Good idea," he agreed. "I'm sure she'll

understand. And when you've done that, give your sister a call. Just to put your mind at ease."

Gina shot him a startled look.

Craig smiled at her fondly. "It's not only twins who can read minds. Husbands can manage that trick once in a while, too. Go on, I hate to see you worrying."

Jody frowned. "Why are you worried about Aunt Maria, Mom?" she asked.

Gina reached up to squeeze Jody's hand. "I'm not really worried. Only, she's been on my mind a lot these past few days, and usually when that happens it means she's thinking about me, too. But she hasn't answered my last two e-mails, and that's not like her."

"Go on and call her," Craig urged.

Gina nodded. "Okay. But I'll write to Alicia Levy first."

Thinking about the link between her mother and Aunt Maria, Jody wondered what it would be like to have a twin. She turned to look down at the far end of the cabin where her brothers, Sean and Jimmy, were building a model racing car. The two boys, also identical twins, did practically everything together. It was hard to imagine them even in separate rooms for very long, let alone grown up and leading separate lives, like her mom and Aunt Maria.

Jody went back to her cabin to put away her diary and change out of her wet clothes. When she returned to the main cabin she saw that her mother was gone, and Dr. Jefferson Taylor had joined her father and the captain to discuss their travel plans.

Dr. Taylor worked for PetroCo, the big corporation that had provided most of the funding for the Dolphin Universe project. However, the funding had come with a catch — a PetroCo representative had to be included on the voyage. It turned out to be Dr. Taylor. But even after two months on board *Dolphin Dreamer,* the awkward, rather old-fashioned scientist still didn't seem to fit in. Nobody really knew what he should be doing — not even Dr. Taylor himself!

Jody realized that Dr. Taylor was now objecting to her parents' plans to move on.

"Aren't there some other scientists we should visit here in the Bahamas?" Dr. Taylor asked. "I'd rather visit more research facilities instead of chasing off into the wild blue yonder."

Jody saw a flicker of annoyance cross her father's easygoing face, but he spoke patiently. "May I remind you, Dr. Taylor, that the purpose of this project is to study dolphins in the wild, as well as making contact with other researchers? We've encountered bottle-nosed and Atlantic spotted dolphins in the Bahamas, but in the Eastern Caribbean, for instance, there are nearly a dozen different cetacean species, such as spinner dolphins, Risso's and Fraser's dolphins, not to mention orcas, pilot whales, and sperm whales." As he spoke, Craig pointed out the areas where they might find these species on the map spread out on the table.

Jody caught her breath with excitement. "Really, Dad? We'll see whales, too?"

Her father turned to grin at her. "All you have to do is keep your eyes open. We're bound to meet sperm whales, dwarf sperm whales, and even pygmy sperm whales within the next two or three months. Unfortunately, we'll be too early for the humpback whales. They don't arrive in the Caribbean until January."

"Excuse me," Dr. Taylor said fussily. "But may *I* remind *you* that PetroCo's funding was for Project *Dolphin* — not Project *Whale*!"

Craig took a deep breath and opened his mouth. "Strictly speaking, yes . . ." he began, then broke off, shaking his head. "Okay, Dr. Taylor, you're allowed to ignore the whales. Just concentrate on the half-dozen dolphin species we're likely to see, and I won't test you on anything else."

Jody struggled not to giggle. Dr. Taylor looked confused, as if he couldn't figure out whether he should feel pleased or insulted by what Craig had said.

Just then, Gina came back in. She was holding the cell phone and gazed anxiously at her husband. "I tried Maria at work, but they said she'd called in sick; when I tried her at home there was no answer."

"Maybe she's at the doctor's," Craig suggested.

Gina nodded, but Jody could see that she wasn't convinced.

"I'm going to send her another e-mail," Gina decided. "I'll tell her to get in touch, no matter what, as soon as she gets it."

As Gina was typing a message to her sister, Cameron Tucker came down the hatch. He was the first mate, a strong, handsome, very blond young man from Florida.

"The rain's cleared away, and there's a good, strong wind," Cameron informed them. "We won't get a better time for sailing today. What do you say, Cap'n?" He looked at Harry Pierce for his orders.

Harry glanced at Craig.

Craig looked at Gina, who was frowning at the computer screen. "Do you need a little longer?" he asked her.

Gina shook her head and logged off, sighing. "No, I don't want to hold everybody up," she replied. "But I'll want to check my e-mail later."

Craig smiled at her fondly. "Sure. A couple of minutes on-line via satellite hookup isn't exactly going to bankrupt us!" He turned back to Harry. "We're ready whenever you are."

Harry nodded briskly. "Prepare to cast off," he told Cam.

His words acted like magic on Sean and Jimmy, who scrambled toward him. "Can we help?" Jimmy demanded, speaking for them both.

Harry gives the twins their orders!

"As long as you're willing to do exactly as you're told," Harry replied, the twinkle in his eyes softening his gruff tone.

"Aye, aye, sir!" the boys chorused, before scrambling up the hatchway after Cam.

Harry looked at his daughter. "Brittany, would you like —"

11

"No, I'm busy!" she snapped, without looking up from the computer.

"Well, perhaps another time," he said quietly, turning away, his shoulders sagging.

Jody felt sorry for Harry. He was trying his best, but his daughter never seemed to notice. Although in the past couple of weeks Brittany had settled down a little, accepting that *Dolphin Dreamer* would be her home for the foreseeable future, she remained moody and unpredictable. She was furious with her mother for having left her behind when she'd gone to France, so she took her anger out on those around her — especially her father.

Jody followed her parents up on deck. Even if her help wasn't needed, she preferred to be out in the open air. She was hoping to get another sight of the porpoise she had seen in the distance. With any luck, they might meet some dolphins wanting to race with their boat as they sailed away from the island of New Providence.

Under Harry's command, *Dolphin Dreamer* sailed swiftly and steadily through the sparkling, clear blue waters out of the harbor and into the open sea.

Jody caught sight of a school of dolphins, but they were too far away to identify the species. She felt happy to be on the move again and leaned against the side, looking forward to all the new dolphins — and whales — they would soon encounter.

A delicious smell of cooking wafted up to her, and as she sniffed the air, Jody realized she was hungry. She went down to investigate.

"Ah, Jody!" Mci Lin, the cook and engineer, greeted her with a warm smile. "Will you tell the others lunch will be ready in five minutes?"

"Sure," Jody agreed, smiling back at the slender Chinese woman. "Something smells delicious!"

Jody found her mother in the main cabin, at the computer again. "Lunch in five minutes," she told her.

"I'll be finished in two," Gina promised, clicking on an icon. "I just want to check if Aunt Maria has replied yet."

Jody waited, watching her mother.

Then Gina sighed and shook her head. "Oh, well, I guess she hasn't checked her e-mail today. I see Alicia Levy has, though. . . . Wonder what she's got to say?"

13

Gina clicked the mouse again and began reading Alicia's message.

"Do I smell lunch?" asked Craig, coming in and sniffing the air.

Jody smiled and nodded.

"Oh, my . . ." said Gina quietly. "Perhaps we should change our plans and visit Dolphin Haven after all . . ."

"What?" asked Craig, frowning in puzzlement. "What are you reading?"

"An e-mail from Alicia Levy," Jody told him, equally confused.

"What does she write?" Craig asked Gina.

"She says she's very sorry we won't be able to visit," Gina replied slowly, not taking her eyes from the screen. "Because something very special is happening at Dolphin Haven. She's busy around the clock monitoring three of their dolphins. . . ."

"What wrong with them?" Jody asked, concerned.

"They're all pregnant," Gina replied. She looked up at Craig, smiling broadly. "And they're all due to calve in the next few weeks!"

Craig gave a low whistle. "Three pregnant dolphins

in one research facility! All at the same time! That's un-heard of!" He nodded at his wife. "You're right. This we have to see!"

Jody yelped with excitement. "Oh! Could we stay and see the baby dolphins being born?" she asked. She couldn't imagine anything more wonderful.

"You'd better believe it!" Craig said, giving her a hug.

Jody giggled as her father began to dance with her around the cabin.

"There is no way we should miss such an amazing opportunity!" Gina agreed. "To see it all at first-hand . . ." She began to laugh and shake her head. "Why did Matt have to be so mysterious about it? If he'd only *said* . . . Alicia Levy is going to think we are total flakes, one minute saying we can't possibly come, the next telling her we've changed our minds!"

Craig stopped dancing and went over and put his hands on Gina's shoulders. "Just e-mail her back and write that we're on our way," he said decisively. "I'll go tell Harry to set a new course!"

2

August 18 — after bedtime — still in the Bahamas!
Change of plans! Now we're staying in the Bahamas to
see baby dolphins being born! That's something that not
even Mom and Dad have seen. We arrived at the island
of Eleuthera, where Dolphin Haven is based, just after
sunset. Dad said we'd wait for morning before going over
to Dolphin Haven. I can't wait! I'm too excited to sleep!

Brittany is awake, too, and pestering me. This marina
where we've docked is part of a big resort and we can hear
music and sounds of lots of people. Brittany thinks it sounds
like fun. She wants to sneak out and find the party. She

called me a chicken when I said no. But if we got caught we'd be in BIG trouble, and it's not worth it. Mom wouldn't let it go unpunished. I couldn't stand it if I got grounded tomorrow and didn't get to meet the dolphins! (I wonder, should the word be "grounded" when you're living on a boat? It should really be the opposite . . . but "floated" doesn't sound right, either!) Better do a big, fake yawn now and pretend I'm falling asleep so Brittany will be quiet.

After a quick breakfast the following morning, the McGraths, Brittany, Maddie, and Dr. Taylor set off for Dolphin Haven. They had learned that a bus ran every fifteen minutes between the marina, the hotel, and Dolphin Haven. Everyone was excited about the change in plans. Even Brittany was intrigued by the possibility of seeing baby dolphins being born.

When the bus arrived, Jody saw that it was decorated with a large, brightly colored poster of leaping dolphins and the slogan, *Make friends with a dolphin at Dolphin Haven!*

"Cool," Sean said approvingly as Jimmy pointed it out to him.

Jefferson Taylor frowned as he waited to board the bus. "I thought we were going to visit a research facility. That ad makes it look like a tourist attraction!"

"From what we've heard, it's both," Craig replied. "The money to keep it running comes from the paying visitors. But it's not just a captive dolphin show. The public learns about dolphins from experts, and at the same time, important research is being done behind the scenes. It sounds like a reasonable mix."

Dr. Taylor sniffed. "I'll make up my own mind about that," he declared as he climbed on board the bus, puffing slightly with the effort.

Jody saw her parents exchange a look. "Should have waited for him to have that second cup of coffee," Craig muttered, hanging back to let Maddie and the twins board the bus ahead of him.

A few minutes later, the bus driver pulled to a stop. "Dolphin Haven!" he sang out. Then, turning around to look at his passengers, he said warningly, "But you're going to have a long wait. It's still closed. The first show isn't until ten o'clock."

"Thanks, but we're not here for the show — we're here to visit Alicia Levy," Craig replied. "She's expecting us."

"Oh, why didn't you say so?" The driver grinned, and nodded briskly. "Keep your seats. I'll drive around to the staff entrance."

Jody gazed eagerly out of the window, but Dolphin Haven was kept hidden from view by a high wooden fence. Very soon the bus stopped again, and, thanking the bus driver, they all got out.

A young woman with closely cropped hair and a gold nose ring met them at the back gate. "Hi, I'm Tamika," she said with a smile. "I'm Alicia's assistant. You must be Dr. McGrath," she went on, holding out her hand to Dr. Taylor.

Dr. Taylor pulled back, looking offended. "I am Dr. Jefferson Taylor," he corrected her.

"*I'm* Dr. McGrath," Gina said, smiling. "And so is my husband."

Craig stepped forward to shake Tamika's hand. "Dr. Taylor is our colleague," he explained. "I'm sure Gina must have mentioned him in her e-mail to Alicia. . . ." As he spoke, Gina bit her lip, giving her head the tiniest of shakes.

Tamika looked blank, but nodded. "Oh, for sure," she said vaguely. "Sorry . . . whatever . . . will you all please follow me?"

Jody thought that Dr. Taylor still looked annoyed by the simple mistake as he stalked stiffly along the tree-lined path after Tamika. Well, it was his own fault for pushing his way to the front, she thought.

Tamika led them to a long, low, white building. "This is the office block," she explained. "There's a lab at the far end, and there's work space for visiting researchers as well." She opened the door to a bright, cluttered office with a big picture window.

The view grabbed Jody's attention. She could see a great, wide sweep of blue water outside, sparkling in the sun. Wooden jetties and docks broke it up, and as she watched, she saw what had to be her favorite sight in the world. A dolphin leaped free from the water, arced through the air, for a moment was silhouetted against the sky, then plunged down again, out of sight. She waited, hoping it would reappear.

"Jody!" Her mother's voice, touched with exasperation, dragged her attention back into the room.

A tall, darkly tanned woman in a blue T-shirt and shorts with gray-blond hair scraped back in a ponytail

Wow! What a sight!

smiled down at her. "Hi, Jody. I'm Alicia Levy. Great view, huh?"

Jody nodded, feeling herself blush.

"Dan — that's my partner — says we'd get twice as much work done without that window. But I think our real work is out there, so I like to keep it in sight. I'm waiting for the day when I can get a *totally* waterproof and indestructible computer. I might never come indoors again!"

Craig laughed. "You sound like a kindred soul! Where is Dan, by the way?" he asked.

"He's still asleep." Alicia made a rueful face. "I'm afraid we're not seeing very much of each other at the moment — we're taking shifts to keep a close watch on our expectant mothers. The rest of the staff has been very good about helping out, but we're all feeling the strain. We could really use some extra help."

"I'll help!" Jody blurted out eagerly. "Just tell me what to do!"

Alicia looked with surprise from Jody to her mother.

Gina nodded. "That goes for all of us. We'd *love* to help," she said warmly.

Alicia blinked. "Well, that's very kind of you . . . but . . . I thought you were only going to stay for a day or two? It could be two or three weeks before the births. Your first e-mail said you were eager to leave the Bahamas."

Dr. Taylor cleared his throat. "Yes, that was the case. But as *I* pointed out, visiting other research facilities and learning about their work is *far* more important than spending endless days at sea, hoping to stumble on some unusual specimens!"

Jody saw a slight flush appear in her mother's cheeks.

Carefully, Gina replied, "Both aspects of our work are important. But I wrote that e-mail before we knew about your pregnant dolphins. Frankly, the chance to witness a dolphin birth is too good to miss. Everything else can wait. We'd really like to stay for the births, no matter how long it takes. That is, if you'll let us?"

"Let you!" Alicia exclaimed, with an excited laugh. "Are you kidding? You are *so* welcome. . . . We can use all the help we can get, but expert help is even better. Dan's not going to believe our luck!"

"Hey, Dad, we're bored," Sean announced suddenly in a low voice. "Can we go outside and explore?"

Gina frowned. "Sean," she said warningly.

Alicia laughed. "I'm with your son," she said. "We have to have somewhere to keep the files and the computers, but this office is definitely not the high point of Dolphin Haven. Come on, I want to show you around. We'll *all* go exploring!"

"How long have you been here?" Craig asked as they all followed Alicia out of the office.

"Five years," she replied as they stepped out into the open air. They stood still for a moment, admiring the view.

"It's a beautiful setting," Maddie commented.

"Yes," Alicia agreed. "The natural lagoon is just perfect. I've never been happy about the idea of keeping dolphins captive in tanks. Here, where they can live in the ocean and have acres of room to swim around in, it's almost like they're free."

Dr. Taylor cleared his throat. "Excuse me," he said. "But how do you manage to study them? Isn't the point of keeping dolphins to have them confined to a small area while you do your research?"

Alicia gave Dr. Taylor a surprised look. "But not all the time," she objected. "That's not necessary. All dolphins deserve a good quality of life. Don't you agree?" Not waiting for his reply, she turned to the others and explained, "In some ways, their lives here may be even better than in the wild — better food, fewer dangers. In exchange for freedom, wild dolphins run the risk of being killed in fishing nets or by pollution or other human activities. We look after them very well here, and in the long run, the things we learn about them may help preserve and improve the lives of dolphins in the wild, too."

Turning back to Dr. Taylor she added, "We don't have to keep them closely confined because we've trained our dolphins to come to us and to hold still while we examine them. They'll enter a small holding tank on command and let us take measurements, readings, and samples."

"What kind of samples?" asked Brittany, speaking up for the first time. "Like blood samples?"

Alicia nodded.

"And they hold still for that?" asked Dr. Taylor, looking disbelieving.

"Yes, they do," said Alicia. "They trust us, we reward them for doing it — and of course, we don't test their patience by doing it too often! In fact, one current research project here involves analyzing saliva samples — which are easy and completely painless to take — in the hope that we might be able to substitute saliva tests for blood tests in the future."

"That would be useful," said Craig. "What other research projects do you have going on?"

"Well —" Alicia began, then she stopped and looked at Sean and Jimmy, who were fidgeting, and at Brittany, who looked as if she wished she'd never asked her question.

Even Jody was trying not to show her impatience. She was interested in everything about Dolphin Haven — but now she really wanted to meet the dolphins!

Alicia smiled. "I can give you all the details of our work later. I'm sure you're all eager to meet the real stars of Dolphin Haven!"

"But I'd like to hear more details about your research now," said Dr. Taylor.

To Jody's relief, Alicia Levy walked on as if she hadn't heard. She took them down to the water's edge and then along a sturdy wooden jetty that had been built out into the bay.

Jody noticed there were several other jetties besides the one they were standing on.

Alicia lifted a whistle she wore on a cord around her neck to her lips and blew three short blasts.

"How many dolphins do you have here?" Maddie asked.

"Ten," Alicia replied. She gazed out to sea, shielding her eyes from the sun. "Eight bottle-nosed and two Atlantic spotted. The three pregnant females are all bottle-nosed. Ah! Here comes one now!"

Jody peered at the water, looking for the moving shape. Then suddenly she caught sight of not one but two curved fins — two dark-gray dolphins traveling together so closely that they were almost touching.

"It's Bella, with Lola," Alicia said. She crouched down on her heels and, as the dolphins swam up and poked their heads out of the water, she reached out to stroke the bigger one. "Hello, darling." The smaller dolphin nudged at her hand and gaped her mouth. She made a chattering sound, almost as if she was telling Alicia off, Jody thought.

Alicia laughed. "Sorry, Lola, I didn't mean to snub you!"

"Are these two related?" Gina asked, gazing down with a smile on her face at the two sleek animals.

Alicia nodded, "Bella is Lola's mother. Lola is nearly five years old."

Jody saw Brittany frown slightly as she stared down at the mother and daughter dolphins. "Is Lola pregnant, too?" she asked.

Alicia shook her head. "Oh, no. We'd be very worried if she was . . . although she is an adult, she's still awfully young to be a mother!"

"How old is Bella?" Jody asked, crouching down beside Alicia.

"She's twenty-six. She had her first calf when she was thirteen, her second five years later, then Lola was born three years after that. It's usual for there to be a gap of anywhere from two to five years between pregnancies," Alicia explained.

"Why so long?" Jody asked.

"Probably because the young dolphin needs so much care and attention," Alicia told her. "They're a bit like baby humans — unlike a lot of animals, they're helpless for a long time after birth. Since male dolphins don't have anything to do with raising their young, the mother doesn't have the energy for anything else until her baby is at least two years old."

"How would they cope with twins?" Jody wondered aloud. She noticed her brothers roughhousing dangerously near the water. Her father called out a sharp warning to them to behave and headed in their direction to prevent any trouble.

"Twins are born very rarely," Alicia replied. "And they die soon after birth. To our knowledge, they've never been known to survive."

"How sad!" Brittany exclaimed.

Jody was surprised, since Brittany was often rather

indifferent to dolphins, and judging by the expression on her face, it seemed that Brittany had even surprised herself.

"It's nature's way," said Maddie quietly.

"Yes," Gina agreed. "It seems sad to us, but it's actually better for the mother — and the survival of the species in general — if twins, or particularly weak calves, die soon after birth. It's no good if the mother wears herself out trying to keep them alive and ends up dying herself!"

"We don't know very much about birth in the wild," Alicia added. "But it seems likely that a large percentage of young dolphins don't survive their first few months of life. Here at Dolphin Haven, we can give them a safe start and a much better chance of survival. But of course, we can't do everything. There are no guarantees." She bit her lip, and a worried frown appeared on her face.

"Are you worried about Bella?" asked Gina.

"Oh, no!" The frown disappeared. Alicia smiled fondly at the pregnant dolphin. "No, Bella is a good, strong, experienced mother. She's been getting plenty to eat, and we're keeping an eye on her, just in case. There's no reason in the world to expect any trouble with her."

Alicia straightened up and peered out to sea again. She blew a few more blasts on her whistle.

Jody followed the direction of her gaze and saw several more dolphins approaching the dock.

"Here they come now," said Alicia. "These are the ones we're a little bit worried about. Misty, because she's young and small and this is her first pregnancy; and Evie. Evie is thirty-two, which is a rather advanced age. She's been pregnant several times before, but she's never managed to give birth to a live calf."

Jody stared up at Alicia's face, shocked.

"Evie and Misty both are going to need all the help we can give them," Alicia went on softly. "And even then, it may not be enough."

3

Jody gazed down at the two dolphins approaching the dock. One of them was enormous. It must have been close to four yards long, Jody guessed, and bulky, too — probably the biggest bottle-nosed dolphin she'd ever met. The other one looked like a baby by contrast, small and slim.

"Are they mother and daughter, too?" Brittany asked curiously.

Alicia shook her head. "The big one is Evie. She's the one who's had a number of miscarriages over the years and never a live birth. But we're determined that this

32

time is going to be different, aren't we, big girl?" She stretched out her arm. The larger dolphin surged up out of the water to bump her head against Alicia's hand, then sank back below the surface with barely a splash.

Jody's attention turned to the smaller dolphin. "This one must be Misty," she said.

At the sound of her name, the young dolphin darted away, then shot out of the water. Her body made a graceful arc in the air before she dived back beneath the surface. Then she circled around underwater and came up alongside the dock, whistling and chattering as if to ask her audience what they thought of *that*!

Looking at the way the dolphin seemed to smile made Jody smile back. "She's gorgeous!" she exclaimed happily.

"She is kind of cute," Brittany agreed, sounding surprised. She moved closer to Jody for a better look. "She's got such beautiful, big eyes!"

"And doesn't she know it!" Alicia exclaimed, laughing. "She's a flirt. Everybody loves Misty. She's always the star of the show."

As if to prove it, Misty whizzed away to perform several more graceful leaps and dives. Then she returned to Evie's side and popped in and out of the water several times, whistling and clicking loudly.

"Are you sure she's pregnant?" Gina asked, smiling at the young dolphin's antics.

"Oh, yes, we're sure," Alicia confirmed, smiling, too.

"How can you tell?" Jody asked, staring at Misty's slim, sleek form.

"Through the wonders of modern technology," said a gruff, male voice.

Startled, Jody turned to see a stocky man in a gray T-shirt and shorts approaching. He was barefoot, his dark brown hair was uncombed, and he looked like he needed a shave.

"Why aren't you in bed?" Alicia exclaimed.

"What kind of a welcome is that?" the man grumbled. "And you don't even introduce me to our visitors. . . ." He turned to Craig. "Man to man, do you get the impression my wife is ashamed of me?"

Jody noticed that, despite his grumpy tone, the man had a mischievous grin, and his brown eyes were warm and friendly.

Misty puts on a show!

Alicia shook her head, but she was smiling. "Meet my husband, Dan Levy, eminent marine mammal veterinarian — though you'd never think it to look at this scruffy guy!" She kissed his cheek and quickly introduced everyone.

Dan shook everybody's hands. When he got to Jody he said, "To answer your question, we know that Misty, Evie, and Bella are pregnant because we've given them ultrasound scans. Otherwise it would be very hard to tell, since pregnant dolphins don't have 'bulges' like many mammals — including people!"

"It was an ultrasound scan that showed I was having twins and not just one baby," Gina said, looking at Sean and Jimmy. "It was so amazing, getting a picture, made by sound waves, of the two tiny babies, curled up inside me."

"Oh, yuck!" Jimmy exclaimed loudly. Sean, bright red, pretended to throw up.

Dan chuckled. "It's kind of interesting that we can now learn more about dolphins through ultrasound, since that's one of the key ways they get information themselves," he explained.

Alicia nodded in agreement. "Until recently it was practically impossible to know if a dolphin was pregnant until she actually gave birth," she said. "But there's been a lot of groundbreaking research done in the last few years —"

"A lot of it right here at Dolphin Haven," Dan interrupted proudly.

"— and now we can even get a good estimate of how far along they are and predict when they're due to give birth — within a few weeks, that is," Alicia concluded.

"You can't get any more exact than that with people, either," Gina pointed out.

"How long is a dolphin pregnancy?" Jody asked.

"Nearly a year for the bottle-nosed," Alicia replied. She turned to look at the four female dolphins who were now swimming away from the dock, as if bored with the humans' conversation. She seemed deep in thought for a moment. Then she turned back to her husband and said, "Dan, I think it's time to move them all into the nursery pool."

He raised his eyebrows. "Seems kind of early to me. I'd be surprised if Evie was ready to give birth much before mid-September, and Misty still has two or three weeks to go —"

Alicia shook her head. "I'm worried about Misty," she interrupted, an anxious frown on her face. "She's still such a baby herself. And I'm sure she's underweight."

"We can't exactly force-feed her," her husband pointed out gently.

"No, but she might calm down a little, not burn up so much energy, in a smaller space," Alicia argued.

Dan nodded thoughtfully. "You're right." Then he added, "But that's an argument *against* moving Evie into the nursery pool. Her problem is the opposite of Misty's. We need to get her fitter, not fatter."

"Couldn't you move Misty into the nursery pool and let Evie stay out here until she's ready?" Gina asked.

Jody thought her mother's suggestion was a sensible one. She was surprised to see both Alicia and Dan shake their heads.

"Oh, no, we can't break them up!" Alicia exclaimed.

"Even before their pregnancies, Bella, Misty, and Evie spent most of their time together," Dan explained. "Now, they're even closer. In human terms, they're family. They look after one another. They'd be lonely and unhappy if we separated them, and that wouldn't be good for their health or for the welfare of their calves! That's why we decided that they should all go into the nursery pool together. Lola, too, since she's still so attached to her mother."

Jody realized that so far, all the talk had been of Misty and Evie, not of Bella. But Bella was pregnant, too. No one seemed concerned about her, because she was so fit and healthy. "When is Bella's baby due?" she asked.

"That was just the point I was about to make," Alicia said, smiling at her husband.

Dan nodded his understanding. "A good point," he said. "If we've judged it right, Bella should be the first to give birth. And it should be this week."

"Which means it's high time we moved her into the nursery pool," Alicia said, looking relieved. "So they'll all go in today."

Dan scratched his chin and said, "We'll deal with Evie's condition by starting her on a strict exercise program. We mustn't let her get lazy. Someone will have to get her through her exercises at least twice a day."

"And at the same time," Alicia said, "we'll have someone else encouraging Misty to be calmer and to eat more." She smiled cheerfully at her visitors. "I'm certainly glad we've got so many extra volunteer helpers now — I hope you won't mind if we take advantage of you!"

"I don't mind!" Jody exclaimed enthusiastically.

"We'll do whatever you tell us," Gina said warmly, moving to put her arm around Jody.

"I guess I could help, too," Brittany said, a little uncertainly.

Jody looked at Brittany, surprised. She wasn't usually so eager to help. And she didn't look as if she was sure she should have volunteered this time.

But Alicia and Dan smiled their thanks, and one of Brittany's own rare smiles broke through. "You'll have to tell me what to do, though," she added. "I'm not really used to looking after animals."

Alicia nodded. "Of course — don't worry about it!" she said warmly.

"And I'll be glad to help, too, of course," said Dr. Taylor. "But I must admit, I'd rather not spend any more time in this hot sun." His round face was flushed pink, and he mopped his brow with a handkerchief. "Can't we do something indoors?"

"Oh, I'm sorry," Alicia exclaimed. "Let's go back up to the office, and we can sit in air-conditioned comfort while we plan our day."

As they all began to follow Alicia and Dan back along the dock, Jody turned to Brittany with a teasing smile. "At least you know now that dolphins are mammals," she said. She remembered that when they'd first met, Brittany had actually thought that dolphins were fish!

Brittany blushed. "That makes me better than you, then," she snapped. "*You* seem to think dolphins are people!"

Jody stared at her in dismay. "Hey, I was just kidding," she said apologetically. "I didn't mean . . ."

But Brittany, her face stony, hurried past without listening.

Jody sighed. Brittany had to be the moodiest girl she'd ever met!

*   *   *

As they reached the office block, they met a short, muscular, fair-haired man.

Alice introduced him as Chip Shannon. "Chip's the chief animal trainer here," she explained.

"You'll have to excuse me," he said with a polite nod. "I'd love to stay and chat with you guys, but I've got a show in five minutes."

"A show!" exclaimed Sean. "What kind of a show?"

Chip grinned at the two boys. "The greatest show on earth," he said. "A dolphin show! They have got to be the greatest acrobats in the animal kingdom! And this isn't just an ordinary show where you watch them do tricks — oh, no! Here at Dolphin Haven, I tell you why we think dolphins behave the way they do, and how a good trainer — that's me," he added proudly, pointing a thumb at his chest, "tries to understand the dolphin mind. I demonstrate how I teach them new games using my knowledge of their natural behavior. And if you're *really* lucky" — he lowered his voice dramatically and bent down closer to the twins, as if sharing a great secret — "I just might let you help me!"

The two boys stared at Chip as if they were hypnotized.

"So, would you like that?" Chip asked, straightening up.

"We sure would!" said Jimmy loudly, his face alight.

"Can we go, Mom? Please?" begged Sean.

Gina frowned slightly. "Not by yourselves. Maybe later, when your dad or I —"

"I could go along and keep an eye on them," Maddie suggested.

"You don't have to, Maddie," Gina replied. "It's very kind of you to offer, but . . ."

"Honestly, I wouldn't mind," Maddie insisted. "In fact, this show sounds kind of interesting. . . . I wouldn't mind seeing it."

Chip gave Maddie a slow grin. "Great! I could really use a beautiful assistant to help me with the show," he said.

Maddie laughed. "Save your flattery for the dolphins," she said. "I'm perfectly happy with the job I've got!"

"Maybe you and Brittany would like to go and watch the show, too, Jody," Gina suggested.

43

Jody shook her head. "No, I'd like to see it sometime, but I'd rather stay and find out how we can help with Bella, Misty, and Evie right now."

"Me, too," mumbled Brittany, reluctant to be seen agreeing with Jody.

Chip had heard the conversation. "What's up?" he asked, looking at Alicia and Dan intently. "Has one of them started —"

Dan shook his head. "Not yet," he said. "But since Bella's less than a week from her due date, we've decided to move all four girls into the nursery pool."

Chip looked relieved. "Good. It'll be easier to keep an eye on them there. I wish I could help — look, I'll send Diego back to give you a hand."

"But don't you need him to help you in the show?" Alicia asked, frowning slightly.

Chip grinned, glancing at Maddie. "I *do* need an assistant . . . but maybe I'll get lucky and somebody from the audience will volunteer?"

"I will!" shouted Sean and Jimmy at the same time, jumping up and down on either side of him.

Maddie laughed. "There you go," she said, chuckling. "An offer you can't refuse! Two for the price of one."

The nursery pool was an area at one end of the lagoon that had been fenced off from the rest. The part of it closest to the dock was shallow. Looking down into it, Jody guessed the water in there was less than a yard deep.

Dr. Taylor had decided to stay indoors and read through a stack of papers about recent research projects carried out at Dolphin Haven, but the McGraths and Brittany had followed Alicia down to the nursery pool, eager to help her with the dolphins.

They were joined by Diego, a boy of about sixteen, wearing swimming trunks. He nodded shyly when Alicia introduced him to everyone but didn't say a word. Moments later he was in the water, swimming strongly away from the dock.

"Is he going to get the dolphins?" Brittany asked, watching him go.

Jody bit her lip to stop herself from grinning. Did

Brittany imagine Diego was going to politely ask the dolphins to follow him, or round them up and drive them like a herd of sheep? she thought.

"He's going to open the gates," Alicia explained. "The dolphins will swim in when I call them, and then Diego will close the gates again."

"That's very low-tech," said Craig, sounding surprised. "Shouldn't you have something electronically operated, so you could open and shut it from the shore?"

"Well, maybe," said Alicia. "But we had to create this nursery pool in a hurry when we found out we had three pregnant dolphins on our hands. It was a lot quicker and easier to build a simple gate ourselves than to send off-island for specialists and expensive equipment." As she spoke, she sat down on the dock and lowered herself into the shallow water.

"Ah, it looks like I won't even have to call them today," she said. "They must have noticed Diego opening the gates. . . . Here they come!" she exclaimed, a big smile on her face.

Jody gazed into the pool. She caught her breath when she saw the four sleek shapes speeding toward them.

46

The four dolphins surfaced in a circle around Alicia, small, explosive sounds coming from their blowholes. She greeted them all by name and murmured, "You good girls are going to stay in this pool for a while, okay? We'll be able to keep an eye on you, and you'll be safe from those bad boys out there."

Jody felt a clutch of anxiety. "What bad boys?" she asked.

Alicia looked across at her, making a rueful face. "Oh, don't pay any attention to my silly baby talk," she said.

"Perhaps one of your reasons for having a separate nursery area is to keep the calves safe from the male dolphins?" Gina guessed.

Alicia nodded. "Just in case," she replied.

Brittany gasped. "The males wouldn't hurt the babies, would they?" she asked, staring at Gina and Alicia.

Jody was horrified. Her first dolphin friend had been Apollo, a male bottle-nosed. She found it hard to believe that friendly, gentle Apollo would harm another dolphin — certainly not a helpless little baby! She, too, looked at Alicia and her mother, hoping for reassurance.

Alicia looked uncomfortable. "We don't really know," she admitted. "I read an article that suggested they might, so we're not taking any chances. But I've never seen any hard evidence to back up the theory."

"Neither have I," Gina added firmly.

Jody felt a little better hearing that. "But why would somebody think dolphins would do something so horrible?" she asked.

"Honey, I know you like to think of dolphins as being gentle and friendly creatures," Gina told her. "And that is the way people generally experience them. But you know dolphins are more complicated than that. They do fight with one another and hurt one another. Sometimes they even kill members of their own species."

Jody nodded slowly, thinking about it. "Like people," she concluded.

"In some ways," her mother agreed.

"We do know that the male dolphins don't have anything to do with raising or protecting their young," Alicia went on. "So there's no reason for them to be around for the birth. Mothers with young calves in the wild band together with other adult females, who help ward off sharks and other predators. They also make male dolphins keep their distance while the calves are young and helpless. So there's obviously some instinct at work. Even if our males are no threat, the mothers will feel happier away from them."

Diego came swimming back just as Alicia finished speaking. "I've closed the gate," he told her, panting slightly. "What should I do now?"

"Thanks, Diego," Alicia said, flashing him a quick smile. She pushed away one of the dolphins who was nudging at her hip. "I'd like you to give Evie some exercise. Nothing too strenuous, though. Avoid high leaps and belly flops. Dolphins are well padded, but remember, our Evie has a history of miscarrying her calves. We don't want her to start labor prematurely!"

"Yes, ma'am, I won't forget," Diego replied, his dark eyes very serious. "How about a ball game?" he suggested.

Alicia looked pleased. "That sounds good!" She looked

at Jody and Brittany, who were watching everything with great interest. "Would you girls like to join in?" She beckoned them to come into the water.

"You bet!" Jody said enthusiastically.

But Brittany didn't look so sure. "I didn't bring my swimsuit!" she said.

"Me, neither," Jody replied. "So, we go in in our clothes!" She wanted to jump into the water with the dolphins right away — but she looked at her mother to make sure it really was okay.

Gina nodded, smiling. "Sure, go ahead."

Brittany looked at Gina in surprise.

"You'll dry off soon in this heat!" Gina said to her, smiling.

But Brittany still didn't look convinced.

Jody took off her shoes and slipped into the water. She looked up at Brittany, who was still standing indecisively on the side. "Come on, Brittany," she said. "It'll be fun!"

Brittany paused for a second longer, then bent to take off her shoes. She took a deep breath. "Okay," she said. "Here I come!"

4

August 21 — morning.

I received an e-mail from Lindsay just now. Today is the first day of school at home! I can't believe it . . . I felt a little homesick and lonely, thinking about Lindsay and Devon and Maria sitting together at lunchtime and talking about their new teachers. I'm not going to mention it to Mom in case she decides it's time our vacation was over! So far, she hasn't said anything about when our formal "home schooling" is going to start — but I sure hope it isn't until after all the dolphin calves have been safely born! I want to be there for the births! I am so excited — I *can hardly stand to be away from Dolphin Haven in case I miss something.*

The cabin door burst open.

"Hurry up, slowpoke!" Brittany exclaimed, poking her head inside. "What are you *doing*? Everybody else is ready to go!"

Jody jumped up, pushing her diary and pen into her day pack along with her swimsuit. "Just coming," she gasped, scrambling for her shoes. She was determined to keep her diary up to date, but it was hard to find a spare moment. She'd written almost nothing about Dolphin Haven because she'd been so busy with the dolphins there.

"You haven't even brushed your hair," Brittany said, regarding her critically. "Here." She thrust a hairbrush into Jody's hand and waited while she gave it a few hasty swipes. "What *have* you been doing?" she demanded.

Jody opened her mouth to explain about the diary, but Brittany shook her head impatiently. "Never mind," she interrupted. "Just come on!"

Although they hurried, they reached the bus stop just in time to see the dark blue bus rolling away. The twins groaned loudly.

"We promised to help Chip with the dolphins before the first show!" Jimmy exclaimed. "Now we'll be late!"

"It's still early," their mother assured them. "And there'll be another bus in fifteen minutes."

"Oh, great," Brittany muttered. "I just love waiting around with nothing to do."

Jody felt guilty for making them all late. Then she remembered something. "We don't have to wait," she said. She dug into her day pack and found the map Alicia had made for her. "Look, there's a shortcut away from the main road, along the beach. Alicia said it shouldn't take more than ten minutes to walk," she finished happily.

Everyone looked more cheerful. Craig looked at the map and pointed out the right direction. "Follow me!" he said.

Only Jefferson Taylor, already seated on the bench by the bus stop, shook his head. "If you don't mind, I'll just wait for the bus," he said. "I had so much to eat for breakfast — Mei Lin is a good cook! — that I'd like to sit and digest my food for a little while."

"That's fine," Gina told him. "We'll see you later."

Craig grinned. "Just make sure you don't get so comfortable that you fall asleep and miss *all* the buses!" he added.

"No, I certainly won't do that!" Dr. Taylor replied, looking very serious.

Jody exchanged a grin with her mother. Dr. Taylor never seemed to know when he was being teased!

The walk took them through a grove of palm trees, their leaves rustling and clattering in the breeze, and then along the white, sandy beach. Jody gazed out at the brilliantly blue sea and happily breathed in the warm, salty air. It might be quicker to take the bus, but she decided that as long as the weather stayed nice, she'd rather go this way.

As they walked, Sean and Jimmy talked about how they would help Chip and what tricks the dolphins could do. They were full of plans.

"When we get home, I mean when we're living in a

house again and not on a boat, I want to get a dog," Jimmy announced. "I'm going to use all this stuff I'm learning from Chip. It'll be the smartest dog in the world!"

"When I get older, I think I might be a lion tamer," Sean decided. "Or maybe I'll train horses! For rodeo riders. Yeah, that would be good."

Brittany gave them a scornful look. "Just because you've learned a little bit about teaching dolphins doesn't mean you'd be any good with other animals," she objected.

"Yes, it does," Sean argued. "Chip said so. He's teaching us the basic rules for training all animals. Although it's much harder to teach animals that aren't as smart or . . . or something else . . . what was it? . . . as dolphins are."

Jimmy provided the missing word. "Social," he said. "Dogs are like dolphins in that way — they're easy to teach because they're smart and they like people. Lions would be much harder because they don't like people so much."

"Yeah," Sean agreed. "And sharks would be just about impossible!"

"They like people, but only to eat," Jimmy agreed.

Jody burst out laughing.

Sean and Jimmy stopped and stared at her, looking wounded.

"What are you laughing at?" Jimmy demanded.

"If you saw the show you wouldn't laugh at us!" Sean said with a scowl.

"I'm sorry — it was just the thought of somebody trying to train a shark," Jody explained, struggling to keep a straight face.

"Chip puts on a good show with the dolphins," Maddie said. "He has a pretty high opinion of himself, but I have to admit it's an impressive display. One of the best I've seen. The dolphins are obviously enjoying themselves as well as wanting to please Chip. He really seems to speak their language! And he's got a real knack for keeping the audience on the edge of their seats."

"Plus you can learn a lot from Chip," Sean added.

Maddie nodded. "Yes. . . . A lot of dolphin displays

bill themselves as educational, but I think this one genuinely is."

Jody was interested. She knew a lot about dolphins already but was always eager to learn more. "I might come see one of the shows today," she told her brothers.

"Sounds like a good idea to all of us," said Gina.

Alicia was in the office with her assistant, Tamika, doing some paperwork. She smiled as the McGraths came in.

"We've just been drafting a schedule," Alicia explained. "I thought we'd divide the day into two-hour watches and take turns. That way the dolphins will never be left alone, but nobody will have to watch for too long. You volunteers can choose the times that suit you best. Dan and I are happy to take the late shifts."

"I don't suppose you'll have people falling over themselves to take the two to four A.M. shift," Craig said with a wry grin.

"Chip, Tamika, and a couple of other staff members have already volunteered to take turns on night watch so we can get some rest," Alicia replied.

"None of us would mind the occasional late night," Gina offered.

"I wouldn't mind," Jody said eagerly.

"I didn't mean you kids," said Gina, giving her a stern look. "You need your rest!" She turned back to Alicia. "What would you want us to do?"

"Just keep an eye on our mothers-to-be," Alicia explained. "Look out for any unusual behavior."

"Like what?" Jody asked curiously.

Alicia shrugged. "To tell you the truth, I'm not really sure! A loss of appetite is one thing we watch for. . . . Otherwise, I'm counting on instinct and observation, I guess . . . a kind of 'feeling' that something is different. If one or more of the dolphins seemed especially restless or seemed to be in distress, that would be a good enough reason to call us out of our beds!"

"And us, if we're not here," Gina said. "Alicia, if you don't promise to phone us at the very first sign, I'm warning you, we'll bring our sleeping bags tomorrow and camp out on the deck until all three births are over!"

Alicia laughed. "Don't worry, we won't forget you! Give me your cell phone number and I'll program it in. . . . Then, if you're on your boat when it all starts happening, I won't have to waste time looking up your number. One press of a button, and you'll get the message." She picked up the cordless phone from her desk. "All staff members have these while they're on the premises. If you press 1, they'll all ring — you can just tell the first person who answers what's up." She paused and frowned as she gazed around the room. "Why do I have the feeling somebody is missing?" she asked.

"Dr. Taylor," said Craig. "He should be here any minute."

"Oh, yes." Alicia nodded. "Well, when Dr. Taylor arrives —"

"Right here," said a familiar voice, and Dr. Jefferson Taylor came through the doorway, panting slightly. There was a broad smile on his round face. "How kind of you to wait for me to arrive before beginning the briefing," he said. "Please! Don't let me delay you any longer!"

"Okay," Alicia said, shrugging slightly. She quickly repeated what she'd told the others and explained the watch system.

"Obviously, you'll want to spend a good amount of time near the pool, watching the dolphins firsthand, but if it's raining or too hot you can see a lot just by sitting in here," she finished, pointing to the closed-circuit television monitor.

"Very sensible," Dr. Taylor nodded. "Very efficient. Well . . ." He looked down at the schedule. "Ah, I see no one has signed up yet. May I have the honor of being first?"

"Go ahead," said Alicia, smiling.

Dr. Taylor bent over the desk and signed his name on the paper with a smile. He handed it to her.

Alicia looked surprised. "You really want to be here that early?"

Dr. Taylor looked startled.

Jody got the distinct impression that he hadn't realized what time he'd actually signed up for. If so, however, he obviously didn't want to admit he'd made a mistake.

"Yes . . . yes, certainly . . . why not? Before the worst heat of the day. I'll be here tomorrow, six A.M., sharp!" he blustered.

"I'll take the next watch," Gina said, reaching for the paper. After she had filled in her name, it was quickly passed around to everyone else. Jody chose the four to six P.M. watch.

"Come on, let's go see how they're doing," Alicia said at last, and they all followed her outside and down to the nursery pool.

Dan was there, crouching in the water. Jody recognized the big dolphin beside him as Evie. She was resting quietly while Dan listened to her heart with a stethoscope.

Dan finished and straightened up as they approached. "Good girl," he said, stroking Evie's side. "Okay, go!" He clapped his hands sharply to emphasize the command.

Evie rolled over in the water and shot away beneath the surface.

Jody saw her join the other three dolphins, who were waiting in the deep end of the pool.

"How are they?" Alicia asked.

"They all seem fine," Dan answered cheerfully. He waded to the edge of the pool. As he took off his stethoscope, he continued, "I'm especially pleased

Dr. Dan checks out his patient.

with Evie's heart rate and breathing. And Misty has calmed down. You know, I think they all feel safer here in this pool, away from the other dolphins."

"Of course they do," Alicia said. "And won't the first baby to be born be lucky to have so many aunts to help with its care!"

"Are they all sisters?" Jody asked, surprised.

Alicia shook her head. "No, it's more an honorary

term. Dolphin females form groups and help one another out. One dolphin will play the role of midwife during the birth, and most dolphin mothers have one or two friends to help take care of the calf after it's born. Sometimes they're relatives, but we refer to dolphin 'aunts' because of the role they play. I guess you could call them nannies or baby-sitters, too," she added with a smile.

"And that means that even though Misty is completely inexperienced when it comes to babies, she's got a better chance to get it right because she'll have Bella and Evie close by. Although Evie hasn't been a mother herself yet, she was around when Lola was born and helped Bella with the birth. So between them, they should be able to give Misty all the help she needs," Dan explained.

They all gazed out at the close-knit group of dolphins at the far end of the pool.

"It's a sobering thing for a vet to have to admit," Dan said quietly, "but there's only so much we can do. When it comes right down to it, what the dolphins need most is one another . . . and a bit of luck, too."

*   *   *

That afternoon, Jody went with her parents and Brittany to *Meet the Dolphins — With Chip Shannon!*

Since Maddie had seen it before, she stayed behind to help Alicia keep an eye on the dolphins in the nursery pool. Dr. Taylor had announced loftily that he had no interest in "tourist attractions" and would rather spend his time reading yet more research papers. Jody wondered if the air-conditioned office, rather than the research, might be the real attraction!

There was a crowd of about twenty people waiting on the dock when they arrived. Jody spotted Sean and Jimmy, each now sporting a bright blue Dolphin Haven T-shirt just like the one Chip Shannon wore. Her brothers were keeping amazingly still, watching Chip as if waiting for his signal to spring into action.

Chip, who had been bent over rummaging in a big plastic crate, now straightened up and walked to the end of the dock, nearest the water. He stood quietly for a moment, looking at his audience as if he were counting them. Gradually, conversation died away, until he had everyone's attention, although he still hadn't said a word.

"Welcome to Dolphin Haven," he said in a voice that carried clearly. "Today you're going to meet three of the dolphins who live here. They'll show you some of the games they like to play and I'll tell you a little bit about them. Then you'll each get a chance to meet the dolphins individually."

"Can we get in the water with them?" The speaker was a tall, skinny boy who looked about fourteen.

Chip shook his head. "Sorry. No. You'll have to stay on the dock —"

"No fair! Pa promised we could swim with the dolphins!" burst out another boy, slightly younger and chubbier than the first speaker. "I wanted to ride on one!"

"No one rides the dolphins at Dolphin Haven," Chip told him.

"They do in other places," the boy objected.

Chip nodded. "Some dolphins do choose to let people ride them. But that's the sort of encounter that has to be freely chosen, not forced. Here at Dolphin Haven, our main concern is the health and safety of the dolphins. We have a good reason for not allowing rides. See that top fin, there?" He pointed to one of the dolphins who was watching him from the pool, seeming to listen as intently as the audience.

"We call that the dorsal fin," Chip continued. "There's no bone in it; if it gets grabbed and handled too much, it can be very uncomfortable for the dolphin."

"Just a short ride, then," said the younger boy in a whining voice. "We'll be real careful."

Jimmy, who had been standing quietly to one side, suddenly took matters into his own hands. He stepped forward and shouted at the boy. "Nobody gets to ride the dolphins! Now be quiet and just watch the show!"

From their ripple of applause, it seemed that the rest of the audience agreed with Jimmy.

"Be quiet yourself! I don't want to watch some silly show — we only came here 'cause Pa promised we could ride a dolphin," the younger boy shouted back.

"If you're not satisfied, you can have your money

back," Chip replied calmly. "Just take your tickets back to the entrance and tell them —"

"You bet we will!" the taller boy interrupted, with a sneer. "And we'll tell everybody else not to bother with this place!" He grabbed the other boy by the arm. "Come on, Josh, we're outta here!"

Good riddance! thought Jody, watching them go. From the little sigh that rose from the audience, she guessed that everyone else felt the same way.

Chip grinned wryly. "Anybody else want to leave because they can't be bothered to treat dolphins with respect?"

There were several enthusiastic shouts of "No way!"

Chip's smile became more confident. "Okay, then," he said. "Now that we know the ground rules, let's get on with the show!"

5

August 22 — really early.

It's still completely dark outside. I woke up when I heard Dr. Taylor stumbling around, and I can't get back to sleep. I can hear ropes creaking and the splash of water as Dolphin Dreamer shifts in place, but otherwise it is totally quiet. Everybody else is asleep. Guess I should take this chance to catch up here.

Brittany tries to be so "cool" about everything, but I can tell she's enjoying the dolphins in spite of herself. The more she learns, the more interested she gets. She's nicer to me, too. Maybe we'll even be friends someday. I have to remember not to tease her, though. She is so sensitive . . . and I think her sense of humor is about the size of Dr. Taylor's — in other words, minuscule!

Jody stopped to look at her watch. She sighed. It was still early, although she had been wide awake for *ages*. She had dressed without waking Brittany. Now she was hungry. She decided to tiptoe out of her cabin and down to the galley to find something to eat.

When Jody entered the main cabin she was surprised to find her mother already there. Surprise turned to alarm when she saw that there were tears in Gina's eyes. "What's wrong?" she asked, her stomach twisting anxiously.

"Nothing, honey." Her mother blinked and sniffed and tried to smile. "I was talking to your Aunt Maria and I got a little emotional, that's all."

Jody noticed then that Gina had the cell phone cradled in her lap. "How is she?"

Gina hesitated, biting her lip. Then she said, "Maria's pregnant."

Jody beamed delightedly. "Wow, that's great! I'm going to have a baby cousin!" Then she frowned. Why did her mother look so uneasy? "What's wrong?" she demanded, going to sit beside her. "Aren't you glad? Please tell me!"

"Of course I'm glad for Maria," Gina agreed. Then she took a deep breath and went on. "But you see, honey, Maria's been pregnant twice before and . . . both times, the babies . . . well, died before they were born . . . she miscarried."

"I never knew that," Jody said, shocked. She felt very sorry for her aunt — but also a little hurt that no one had told her about it.

Her mother squeezed her hand. "You were a lot younger then. And Aunt Maria was far away in New York. Losing the babies wasn't something she wanted talked about."

Gina sighed and shook her head. "Anyway, that's why I hadn't heard from Maria," she explained. "She wasn't going to say anything, because she didn't want me to worry. But her doctor thinks that if the baby grows okay over the next few weeks, then everything should be all right this time." Gina finished with a tentative smile.

Then she straightened up and gave Jody a questioning look. "Now, tell me why you're up so early," she said.

"I just couldn't sleep any longer," Jody explained. "I can't stop thinking about Bella and Misty and Evie and wondering if today will be the day!"

"I know what you mean. It's awesome!" Gina said, sharing a smile with Jody. "Bella is due any day now. I certainly would hate to miss the big event. . . . The actual birth can be over in minutes, so as soon as they call, we'll have to move fast!"

"No waiting around for the bus," Jody agreed with a grin.

"There may not *be* a bus," Gina told her. "A lot of births happen at inconvenient times — at night or early in the morning."

Jody caught her breath. She jumped to her feet, suddenly impatient. "What if it's happening *now*?" she cried.

"Alicia did promise to phone us at the very first signs," Gina reminded her.

"I couldn't bear it if I weren't there!" Jody exclaimed.

"Me, neither," said Gina with a sympathetic look. She smiled. "Grab yourself some breakfast and run along over there. I'll get dressed and join you as soon as I can."

"Thanks!" Jody kissed her mother, then dashed to the galley to make a sandwich. She would eat it on the way.

The sun was already up, but everything seemed quiet when Jody arrived at Dolphin Haven. She went right to the office.

As she opened the door she saw Dr. Taylor leaning back in the big chair facing the closed-circuit television. His eyes were closed and his face seemed very thoughtful. Jody frowned uncertainly. She didn't want to disturb him if he was thinking . . . but shouldn't he be keeping a closer eye on the screen? Then, as she stepped inside the room, she heard a snore.

Dr. Taylor was sound asleep!

Jody shook her head in dismay. What was the point of him watching the dolphins if he couldn't even stay awake? If one of the dolphins went into labor, he wouldn't even notice! She looked at the television monitor that showed the nursery pool and was immediately relieved to see there were two people standing beside the pool. If other staff members were up and about, it didn't really matter that Dr. Taylor had dozed off.

But then she examined the figures on the screen more closely. They didn't look like anyone who worked at Dolphin Haven. They were two teenage boys, one tall and skinny, the other somewhat smaller.

Jody frowned. Could they be volunteers? There was something familiar about them.

Suddenly, she remembered where she had seen them before. They were the two boys who had made trouble at Chip's show, wanting to ride the dolphins.

Just as she remembered, Jody saw them move. They jumped into the water of the nursery pool and began grabbing at the dolphins.

Jody gasped, horrified. It was clear that these boys were determined to get their ride, one way or another! "Wake up, Dr. Taylor!" she cried. "We've got to stop them!"

"Wha'?" Mumbling and blinking, Jefferson Taylor began to wake up.

"Where's the phone?" Jody demanded.

The sleepy scientist just blinked back at her in confusion.

Then Jody saw the cordless phone lying on the desk in front of him. There wasn't time to make him understand; she had to act quickly. She grabbed it and pressed "1," biting her lip impatiently as she waited for the connection to be made.

In the meantime, Jody saw from the monitor that the taller boy was now seated on one of the dolphins' backs and that the other was still trying to grab another dolphin. "Come on, Dr. Taylor!" she shouted. "Down to the pool — we have to help!"

Without waiting for his reply, Jody thrust the phone into his hands. "Tell everybody to come quick! It's an emergency!" she said desperately, then rushed out of the building and ran as fast as she could down to the nursery pool.

Jody began shouting at the boys. "Hey! Get out of the water! Leave those dolphins alone!" Her heart was pounding. Now she could see that the bigger boy was riding Evie. The other one was approaching Misty. "You'll hurt them!" she cried, coming closer. "Get away from them!"

"It's only a kid," sneered the older boy. "She can't stop us. . . ."

But as she spoke, Evie suddenly decided she'd had enough. With one flex of her big, powerful body she threw her rider. The boy went splashing into the water with a yell of surprise. In the sudden confusion, Misty slipped away from the other boy.

In moments, the two dolphins were both at the far end of the pool, forming a tight defensive group with Bella and Lola.

Jody breathed a sigh of relief.

"What's going on here?"

The welcome sound of Dan's voice made Jody look around. She saw Dan and Alicia both hurrying toward the pool.

The sight of adults approaching sent the two boys into a flurry of activity. They scrambled out of the water and took off, running without a backward glance.

Evie throws the rider!

"Who were they?" Alicia asked as she reached Jody's side.

Quickly, Jody explained what had happened.

"Probably no point in phoning the police," Alicia said, exchanging a look with her husband. "If they were only kids. But I will inform the hotel — see if they can track down the parents. Jody, could you give me a description of the boys?"

Jody nodded eagerly. "Chip will remember them, too," she said.

"We'll deal with them later," Dan said firmly. His face was grim. "But the first thing to do is check that the dolphins are okay. Evie or Misty could still miscarry . . . if those kids have frightened one of them into premature labor. . . ."

Jody tensed with worry.

Alicia gave her a quick hug. "Thank you for acting so quickly," she said warmly. "There's probably been no harm done. Those boys weren't in the pool for very long — thanks to you! I doubt that the girls were seriously frightened. Our dolphins are all used to meeting people, after all. Even kids who misbehave."

Jody felt a little better. Alicia sounded so confident.

"Just the same, we'll give them each a thorough examination," Dan said. He turned to Tamika, who had just arrived. Jody saw that, in her haste, she'd put her T-shirt on inside out. She'd obviously just come from her bed, yet she looked alert and ready for work.

"Dr. Taylor told me what happened," she gasped. "Are the girls okay?"

"That's what we're going to find out," Alicia told her.

"Would you fetch the ultrasound equipment, please, Tamika?" Dan asked.

As she nodded and dashed off, Dan moved to the side of the pool with his black medical case.

Jody watched anxiously as Alicia and Dan both got into the water and called to the dolphins.

Bella swam straight to Alicia in response to her whistle, but Misty and Evie hovered at the far end of the pool, and Lola was with them.

This struck Jody as unusual behavior. She had noticed that Lola nearly always stayed close to her mother. When Alicia or Dan wanted to examine Bella, they usually had to send Lola away.

Bella lay quietly in the water while Dan checked her out. "She seems fine," he reported. "Heart rate and breathing are both normal. She's not in any distress."

Suddenly, Evie began to swim around the pool. She swam swiftly, circling it again and again.

"What's with Evie?" Alicia asked.

Jody frowned, watching the big dolphin race around. She was making a rapid clicking noise as she went. "One of those boys climbed onto Evie's back and tried to make her give him a ride," she said. "He might have been kicking her — I couldn't see. She was the only one they actually caught. Do you think he hurt her?" She felt sick at the thought.

Tamika arrived and began to set up the ultrasound equipment at the side of the pool. "Are you going to check Bella first?" she asked.

Dan shook his head. He exchanged a glance with Alicia. "I think Bella is fine," he decided. "Healthy as ever, and according to Jody those kids didn't bother her."

"Evie's the one we need to check," Alicia said. "I've never seen her act like this before."

Alicia gave the command that allowed Bella to swim

away. She immediately went to join Misty and Lola at the far end of the pool.

"What have we missed?"

Craig's voice caught Jody's attention. As she looked around she was relieved to see that her parents had arrived, along with Maddie and Brittany. She quickly filled them in on what had happened.

"You mean nobody's having a baby?" Brittany asked, her voice sharp with disappointment. "You mean we hurried all this way for *nothing*?"

"Something's up with Evie," Alicia said.

The worry in her voice caught everyone's attention.

"She's ignoring my call," Alicia explained. "She *never* does that!"

They all stared at the big dolphin, still swimming rapidly around the pool, emitting a steady stream of clicks.

"If she's already in labor, she might not be able to respond to your command," Craig pointed out.

Jody caught her breath with excitement at the thought that a baby dolphin was on the way.

But Dan and Alicia both shook their heads, rejecting the possibility.

"That's not natural behavior for any animal giving birth," Dan explained. "She's using up too much energy. If she felt the baby coming she'd try to relax. Even if she was in pain, I'd expect her to thrash around a bit, but mostly stay in one place. She wouldn't suddenly start patrolling the area like that, as if she was on guard duty —" He broke off as Alicia gasped.

"Of course!" Alicia exclaimed. "If they were in the wild, Evie would be guarding her friend from any outside dangers, like hungry sharks or curious males. Of course! I should have recognized that behavior at once! It's not Evie who's gone into labor —"

"And we know it's not Bella," Dan chimed in.

They all gazed down at the far end of the pool, where Misty was resting, her body just below the surface of the water, sandwiched between Bella and Lola.

"But it's two weeks earlier than we expected," Alicia said softly, her voice strained and anxious. "She's still so small! Oh, I hope it will be all right."

"So what's going on?" Brittany demanded with a puzzled frown.

Jody felt torn between excitement and fear as she understood the situation. Swallowing hard, she turned to Brittany. "It's Misty," she told her quietly. "Misty is having her baby right now."

6

Jody heard her mother say, "Is there anything we can do to help?"

"There really isn't anything we *can* do to help yet," Alicia replied. "We'll just have to let nature run its course."

"It's best if everyone keeps quiet and calm," Dan added. "Misty may be feeling a little frightened right now, and we don't want to do anything that might add more stress."

"Will it be all right if I get a little closer?" Craig asked. He showed Dan and Alicia the compact camcorder he held in one hand. "I'd really like to get the whole thing on video."

"That would be great!" Alicia exclaimed. "I hadn't even thought of doing that! What a brilliant idea. Thank you, Craig!" She beamed at him.

Watching the dolphins, Jody felt so glad Misty wasn't alone. She had her good friends Bella and Lola pressing close to her on either side. They were taking good care of her. Occasionally, Misty would wriggle and make a squeaking sound. When she did this, the other three dolphins replied with a variety of whistles and clicks. Jody imagined they were comforting and encouraging their friend.

Evie must have finally decided that the pool was completely safe, because she gave up her rapid circlings and swam closer to the other three. At this, Bella shifted her position, dropping lower in the water and moving underneath Misty. With her back beneath Misty's belly, Bella pushed the other dolphin toward the surface.

"Why is she doing that?" Jody wondered aloud. "It looks like Bella is holding up Misty."

"Yes, she's helping to support her," Gina explained. "Remember, Misty needs to stay near the surface to breathe. And if she's struggling to give birth she'll find it harder to stay afloat."

"We're lucky that Bella is such an experienced mother," Alicia said quietly, not taking her eyes from the scene in the pool. "She knows exactly what Misty needs and how best to help her. It's just as well that Misty's calf is being born before Bella's, because this way Bella can give Misty her complete attention. I'm sure that having an experienced midwife makes all the difference to a first-time mother."

"Bella can give her more help than we could hope to ourselves," Dan agreed.

The minutes crept past. There was no sign of a calf. As far as Jody could see, nothing had changed. She could feel the tension mounting.

"How long is this going to take?" Brittany asked, fidgeting a little.

"We don't really know," Alicia replied. "Dolphin births are supposed to be quick, compared to humans, at least.

I suppose the labor could take as long as an hour, or maybe longer. There just isn't enough firsthand knowledge to be sure."

Brittany signed. "I wish I'd had breakfast," she muttered.

A few more minutes went by in silence, apart from the steady, soft lapping of the water and the sounds the dolphins made among themselves. Then, suddenly, Dan tensed and leaned forward. "Something's happening," he said.

Misty shuddered and flexed her body.

Alicia gasped. "I can see the tail!" she cried.

Jody stared. Then she saw it, too. For a strange moment, Misty seemed to have two tails, a smaller one growing below her own tail. Seconds later, the smaller tail seemed to grow longer as more of the calf's body slipped out.

Misty's body bent and flexed, pushing her baby out farther. Then, at last, the head emerged, and the newborn dolphin slipped out into the water.

Jody gazed at the sight with awe. The calf looked surprisingly big for a newborn. Jody had expected a much smaller animal, but it was already one-third the size of its mother. She saw that a silvery gray line connected the two and realized this must be the umbilical cord. While the baby was still inside the mother, it would have fed through this attachment.

"Quick, Tamika, hand me the surgical scissors, please," Dan said. "I may have to cut the cord — I don't think Misty knows what to do."

"Wait." Alicia put a restraining hand on her husband's arm. "Bella knows!"

Sure enough, even as she spoke, Bella had bitten down on the cord, safely separating mother from baby.

Evie swam beneath the calf. With Bella beside her, they guided the newborn dolphin to the surface.

As soon as the top of the calf's head was out of the water its blowhole opened, and the young dolphin instinctively breathed in.

A collective sigh rose up from the watchers around the pool.

Tears sprang to Jody's eyes. She felt so relieved that Misty's baby had been safely born.

"We're not out of the woods yet," Dan said quietly, as

Mother and baby are doing fine!

if reading her thoughts. "We don't know yet if Misty will be able to feed her baby. There are some things Bella and Evie can't do for her."

Suddenly, Misty began to whistle. Again and again, she made the same, distinctive sound, while the other adults were silent.

"Is that her signature whistle?" Jody guessed. She knew that although dolphins made lots of different noises to communicate with one another, each dolphin had one distinctive whistle, different from all the others. This was called a "signature whistle" because it was thought dolphins might use it to identify one another, almost like a personal name.

"Uh-huh," Alicia agreed. She was smiling and her eyes were very bright. "Oh, good girl, Misty! You're teaching your baby how to recognize you!" She explained, "Mother dolphins whistle almost continuously for the first few days after a birth. Probably it's so the calf won't ever mistake anyone else for dear old Mom and wander off! And of course, this is how the newborn starts to learn the meaning of different signals."

Jody wondered if Bella and Evie would continue to

guide the baby, but it seemed as though this wasn't necessary. The calf swam back to Misty, as swift and as straight as if she'd reeled it in, as if an invisible line connected the two of them.

Misty rubbed against her baby. She nudged and guided the calf with her flippers and the movements of her body until it responded. It nestled against her, butting and nuzzling at her underside with its beak until it found the hidden teat and began to suckle.

"Well done," said Dan quietly. He and Alicia hugged each other tightly for a moment. Then he looked around at everyone. "Well, folks, I think we should leave the mother and baby alone together to bond," he said. "The calf has been safely born and seems to be feeding well."

"And speaking of feeding," Alicia interrupted, "I don't know about the rest of you, but I am absolutely starving!"

Dan and Alicia cooked breakfast for everyone in their big, sunny kitchen, with a little help from Tamika.

Jody sat beside Brittany at the long wooden table,

feeling very hungry as she waited for the food. She saw Jefferson Taylor wander in. He looked rather sheepish.

"I'm terribly sorry about falling asleep — I can't apologize enough," he began, approaching Alicia nervously.

Alicia cut his apology short with a smile and a shake of her head. "It could have happened to anyone," she said. "And all's well that ends well!" She poured another glass of orange juice. "Here, have one of these! Coffee will be ready in a minute."

"Thank you," Dr. Taylor mumbled, taking a glass. "I just can't believe I fell asleep. I promise you, it won't happen again."

Dan spoke from the other end of the kitchen, where he was scrambling eggs. "I'm sure it won't," he said reassuringly. "It wasn't fair to make you get up so early, and all on your own. From now on, I think you should take a midmorning watch, or maybe one in the early evening. Or — I've got an idea: Maybe we should have two-person watches. How about teaming up with Jody? That worked out pretty well this time!"

Jody just managed to keep herself from groaning out loud at the idea of being stuck as Dr. Taylor's partner

Her dad must have seen the alarm on her face, because he spoke up quickly. "Surely there aren't enough people, Dan? If we all take partners, you and Alicia will soon be bearing the brunt of it again!" He stood up to allow Dr. Taylor to squeeze in beside him as he spoke.

Alicia smiled as she came over to take a seat at the table on the other side of Craig and across from Gina. "We're just about to get some more people," she told them happily. "There's a researcher in Canada scheduled to arrive next week, and we received an e-mail last night from a couple of graduate students in Texas, *begging* for the chance to help out! I told them yes . . . and they're going to come just as soon as they can get flights."

"Some of the support staff have already volunteered to put in extra unpaid hours to keep watch on the newborn dolphins," Dan added. "And I have a suspicion that people who work elsewhere on the island may start volunteering to help once they learn Misty's had her calf." He grinned. "There's something about babies that gets everybody interested."

Brittany looked puzzled. "But why do you need so

many people? Misty gave birth this morning without needing any help — except from the other dolphins."

"Yes, I know," Alicia nodded. "And we're hoping that things will go just as smoothly for Bella and Evie. But when the calf is born, it's only the beginning. The new-born is very fragile. The first month of life will be the most crucial. If there's any problem with nursing, if the calf isn't gaining weight or developing as expected, we may have to step in to help. That's why we intend to keep a very close watch on Misty and her calf around the clock for the next four weeks or so, and we'll do the same with the other two. That's why we need so many volunteers."

Dr. Taylor was frowning. "I hope you don't feel that I'm not to be trusted," he said quietly, staring down at the wooden tabletop. "Keeping watch should be a simple thing, not requiring two people. . . . Please let me show you I can do it. Give me another chance this afternoon. Or —" he winced, swallowed hard, and said, "maybe early evening would be best — before dinner. I have an unfortunate tendency to doze off after

93

meals. . . . Of course, I'll understand if you feel you can't trust me," he finished.

"Of course, we'll give you another chance!" Alicia cried out. She reached across Craig to pat Dr. Taylor's plump white hand. "Honestly, we're just so grateful for your help — you really don't have to do this at all, you know," she told him.

Dr. Taylor looked up and met her clear gray eyes. He nodded. "I want to help," he said fervently.

"Okay," Alicia agreed. "You're on the late afternoon — early evening — shift from now on. It's a deal!"

Dr. Taylor's small brown eyes shone gratefully.

"That coffee must be ready," said Craig, getting to his feet. "Can I pour anybody else a cup?"

Although she was hungry, Jody could hardly wait to get back outside and see the baby again. She felt her heart sink when Alicia said it was important to keep the noise and excitement down around the area of the nursery pool.

"Although we have to keep an eye on them, I really think we should leave the dolphins to themselves as much as possible in the early days," Alicia explained as

everyone dug into plates of eggs, hash-brown pota-
toes, bacon, and English muffins, "so that Misty and her
calf will bond."

"I'm going to check and weigh the calf this afternoon," Dan said. "I also want to check Evie and Bella —
maybe do another scan to make sure they're both all
right after this morning's excitement."

"Can we videotape you while you're doing that?"
Gina asked.

Dan nodded enthusiastically as he spread butter on a
muffin. "Please do! In fact, I think a video diary of the
first weeks of the new calf's life would be a great idea!"

"Can I help?" Jody asked excitedly.

Gina smiled but shook her head. "I don't need any
help, honey," she said. "I'm a one-person camera crew,
remember? Anyway, you heard what Alicia said about
keeping the noise and the crowds down."

Jody sighed. "I wish there were *something* I could
do to help," she said wistfully.

"You could help me get the dolphins' meals ready, if
you like," Tamika offered.

"I'd love to!" Jody nodded eagerly.

"How about you, Brittany?" Tamika asked, turning to the other girl.

Brittany wrinkled her lip. "No, thanks! I'm not crazy about handling dead fish."

Tamika laughed. "It's not *my* favorite thing to do on a full stomach, either, but we can't let the dolphins go hungry!"

"No, we can't," Jody agreed. She looked at Brittany, wondering if she would change her mind.

But Brittany only shrugged. "I guess I'll go back to the boat, then," she said. She smiled. "My dad'll want to hear what happened this morning!"

"Tell Harry to send Sean and Jimmy here if they're any trouble," Gina told her.

After they'd finished eating, Jody followed Tamika out of the kitchen. They went outside, past the office building, along a concrete pathway toward another, separate building made of white concrete.

As they approached it, Jody sniffed the air. It was heavy with the smell of fish. "Hmm, there's something fishy going on," she joked.

"Yes, it's not hard to give directions — I could have told you just to follow your nose," Tamika replied with a smile. She unlocked and opened a set of double doors and switched on the light as she stepped inside.

Jody followed her into a large, plain room with a concrete floor. She saw two enormous chest freezers and wall-mounted cupboards. There was a long counter, gleaming and clean, on either side of a big, deep-basined sink. On another counter she saw several huge plastic tubs full of fish. Below there were rows of brightly colored plastic buckets — at least twenty of them.

Jody walked confidently over and picked up a bucket. She had helped feed dolphins before. "How many buckets should I fill with the fish?" she asked.

"Whoa," said Tamika, laughing. "Not so fast! I know you're eager to help, but feeding dolphins isn't just a matter of throwing them a lot of fish!"

Jody stared in surprise. "It isn't?"

"I'm afraid not," Tamika told her. "We have to carefully weigh and measure it first, to make sure each dolphin gets exactly the amount it needs. We also put vitamin tablets into the fish, so we have to count them out first, too."

This was news to Jody. Last time she'd helped feed dolphins, the buckets of fish had already been waiting at the poolside. She hadn't realized that so much work had gone into preparing them.

Tamika opened one of the cupboards and counted vitamin tablets out of a large plastic container, separating them into piles on the counter.

"Why do you need to give the dolphins vitamins?" Jody asked curiously.

Tamika smiled. "You see, most of the fish we give them has been frozen, and when fish is frozen it loses a lot of its natural vitamins," she explained.

Jody frowned, puzzled. "But why feed them frozen fish? The sea around here is full of fish! We had fresh fish for dinner last night — Harry and Cam caught it themselves, and it was absolutely delicious!"

"There are several reasons," Tamika explained. "If we relied on local fisherman for fresh fish, there would be days when they couldn't go out because of the

weather, and days when they didn't catch enough. . . .
Buying frozen fish means our dolphins never go hungry. Also, it's more economical. And there's another
reason, too."

"What's that?" Jody asked.

"Dolphins especially like oil-rich fish, things like herring and capelin. You don't find them around here;
they come from colder-water regions. So by buying
frozen fish from other parts of the world, we can provide our dolphins with a better, more nutritious diet
than they'd get on their own."

She finished sorting out the vitamins and turned to
Jody. "Before you start, there are some rubber gloves in
that drawer to protect your hands while you handle
the fish." She went on, "Look carefully at each bucket —
only take the ones with names on them. When you've
filled one, take it over and weigh it on the scales over
there." Tamika pointed at the far wall, which was decorated with charts. "Check the name on the chart to see
how much the food should weigh, and either take
some out or add more to get the right amount. Then
bring it to me, and I'll add the vitamins. Okay?"

Jody nodded. She glanced at the charts. "How do you figure out how much each dolphin needs to eat?" she asked.

"That takes a bit of figuring," Tamika admitted, grinning. "I don't deal with that side of it; I leave it to Alicia and her calculator . . . although Dan said something about a new computer program. . . . I know each dolphin gets between five and ten percent of his or her body weight in food every day — but the percentage changes according to how much exercise they're getting, how cold it is, their age and health, and so on."

Jody shook her head in wonder. "Wow, I never thought feeding dolphins could be such a complicated business!" she exclaimed as she lifted the first bucket to the counter and got busy.

7

August 23 — before breakfast.
Me and my big mouth!

I fired off an e-mail to Lindsay yesterday to tell her about Misty's calf. She sent me a really good one back, with lots of gossip about school. There was one really funny story I knew everybody would like, so I told it at dinner. Mom got a funny look on her face — but not from the joke! "You mean, school has already started?" she asked. Gulp! I had to tell the truth. So Mom said we'd better not waste any more time, and if Maddie had her les-

son plans ready, school would start tomorrow. Which is to say, today, because of course Maddie was ready.

The twins started moaning and groaning. Brittany became really quiet and stopped eating. I pointed out that helping out at Dolphin Haven was really educational. But nothing worked. When Mom has made her mind up, that is it.

Anyway, Dad promised that as soon as Bella and Evie go into labor, we'd be allowed to cut class and go right over to Dolphin Haven. And Maddie said there was no way she was going to miss any of the excitement, either! Plus, we have our scheduled hours to do on watch. We won't have to do schoolwork all the time.

Even so, I can't help but feel like these are my last few minutes of freedom . . .

There was a knock on the cabin door. Then Maddie's voice: "Come on, girls, breakfast is ready! No sleeping is allowed!"

With a sigh, Jody stowed her diary and pen away and hopped off her bunk. She turned and looked at Brittany, who was lying on her back, fully dressed except for her shoes. She was just staring at the cabin's ceiling.

"Are you okay?" Jody asked with a puzzled frown.

Brittany sat up abruptly, shaking her head. Her face was sullen. "Don't worry about me," she said flatly. "I'll be okay."

Jody had an uneasy feeling that there was trouble ahead. . . . Something brewing with Brittany, but she decided it was better to say nothing rather than risk making things worse.

Brittany continued to brood over breakfast. She only picked at her food, even though Mei Lin had made her favorite buckwheat pancakes. And as soon as Craig and Gina had headed off for Dolphin Haven and the table had been cleared for schoolwork, Brittany burst out with a complaint.

"How can you teach us all at the same time?" she asked Maddie. "I'm too old to be in a class with *them*." She stabbed a finger at Sean and Jimmy, who were looking well scrubbed and — for once — almost angelic as they sat alertly with new notebooks and pencil cases laid out in front of them.

Brittany went on, "They're third-graders. How can you put us in a class together? I'm supposed to be in the seventh grade, for goodness' sake!" She scowled furiously.

"This isn't going to be exactly like the schools you're used to," Maddie explained patiently. "Think of it as two classes, supervised by one teacher. Sean and Jimmy will have their work, and you and Jody will have yours." She glanced down at the two folders in front of her, one blue and one red. "I'll divide my time between you, but I'm expecting that since you're older, you and Jody will be able to do more on your own, without me standing over you. But I'm always here to help when you get stuck — or you could ask someone else on board to help."

"Even me," Cam added, leaning out of the galley where he was drying the dishes after Mei Lin washed them. He grinned. "I have to confess I'm not as smart as Maddie, but believe it or not, I did go to college — and I'm pretty good with numbers!"

"Cam's offered to introduce the boys to multiplication this morning," Maddie explained.

"What's multiplication?" Sean asked with a suspicious frown. "Is it hard or easy?"

"It's fun," Cam promised.

"It's just the stupid times tables," Brittany said sharply. She made a face at the twins. "And that is *not* fun!"

Sean and Jimmy looked at each other doubtfully.

"Well, it's fun the way *I* teach it," Cam said swiftly. "Wait and see! And when you've learned how to multiply and divide really well, I might even teach you about navigation!"

Jimmy nodded, convinced. "That sounds great — can we start now?"

"Sure," said Cam. "Bring your notebooks and pencils and come outside with me. It's a terrific day, not too hot but not too breezy, either. I'm kind of a noisy teacher, so we'd better find somewhere where we won't bother Maddie's class!"

"Thanks, Cam," Maddie said, smiling up at him. "I couldn't manage without you!" Her voice was warm and affectionate. Jody saw Cam shrug his shoulders awkwardly and blush.

Brittany noticed, too, and gave Jody a wide-eyed, raised-eyebrows look.

Jody was relieved that Brittany seemed to have

snapped out of her bad mood. So she wiggled her eyebrows in reply and saw Brittany's mouth twitch. The girls made goo-goo eyes at each other. Jody had to bite her lip to keep from giggling. But by the time Maddie looked at them, they were both straight-faced and gazing back at her innocently.

The morning passed surprisingly swiftly. Brittany settled down to work without further protest. After half an hour's introduction to algebra, Maddie went off to "rescue Cam," as she put it, and take charge of the twins, leaving Brittany and Jody with a pageful of problems to solve.

Later, while Sean and Jimmy were engrossed in their new workbooks, Maddie gave a history lesson on the American West. She had a lively style, and both Jody and Brittany hung on her words.

Afterward, Maddie showed them the history textbook they would be using. "I'm afraid there's only one copy of each book, so you girls will have to share," she began.

Brittany frowned. "Oh, great! We have to share textbooks, share a computer. . . . What next? Share pencils?"

Jody's heart sank. Why did everything have to be such a big battle with Brittany?

Maddie kept her cool. "Think of it as another lesson — learning to cooperate," she said calmly. "A shortage of things can sometimes make people more resourceful. Now, I'm going to give you a few questions based on what we've just covered. For research, you can use this book, or I have a CD-ROM that covers the same —"

"I have dibs on the computer!" Brittany yelled.

Jody frowned, annoyed. After all, it was her computer. "That's not fair!"

"You may each have half an hour on the computer," Maddie said firmly. "This isn't a big research project; I want your answers, handwritten, before lunch."

Brittany glared sullenly. "I don't like to write. I always type and print out all my homework."

"This isn't homework," Maddie told her. "It's a classroom assignment. Think of it as an open-book test. Each question shouldn't take more than a line or two, at most. The whole thing should fit on the page I give you. Okay? Any questions?"

"Why can't I type my answers?" Brittany demanded.

"They're to be handwritten," Maddie said firmly. "That's the assignment." She handed them each a page with questions printed on it. "I'll leave you to it."

Jody got down to work. As she read through the first chapter of the history book, she soon found it had everything she needed. She began to write the answers on her question sheet. When she had finished, she looked at her watch and was surprised to realize that forty minutes had gone by. "Hey, Brittany," she said, "it's been more than half an hour. . . ."

"I'm not through," Brittany snapped.

"Well, don't you want the book?" Jody asked, keeping her voice friendly.

"No, I don't." Brittany looked away from the computer screen and wrinkled her nose. "You can keep the stupid book. This CD-ROM is much better — you can look up anything you want, and there's photographs, and sound bites from famous people, and videos. . . ."

"Not from the 1800s!" Jody laughed.

Brittany looked at her as if she was crazy. "Who cares about the stupid 1800s?" she asked.

Jody was surprised. "Haven't you been doing the work Maddie gave us?"

"I'll get around to it." Brittany rolled her eyes. "It's not like it's that hard!"

Jody stared at her, disbelieving. "But Maddie said —"

"I know what Maddie *said*," Brittany interrupted. "Who cares!" She turned her attention back to the screen.

Jody felt uneasy. But what could she do? She left her to it and went up on deck.

Harry was seated with the twins on either side of him. Sean and Jimmy were taking turns reading aloud from a book. Harry nodded seriously. He occasionally corrected a word and seemed very interested in the story.

Maddie had been on the other side of the deck, talking quietly with Cam, but when she saw Jody she broke off and smiled at her. "Finished your work already?" she asked, holding out her hand for the paper.

"I have," Jody replied, handing it to her. "But Brittany's still on the computer."

"Well, we can let her have a few more minutes," Maddie said. She glanced over Jody's shoulder. "Hey, look, here comes your mom!"

Surprised, Jody looked around. "Is anything wrong?" she asked her mother as soon as she'd boarded the boat.

"No, of course not," Gina said. But Jody thought her smile seemed strained. "Evie is as big and unbothered as ever. Bella's fine. Misty and the new calf are both thriving, with lots of extra TLC from Bella and Lola. Your dad and Dan are busy analyzing some test results, so I thought I'd come back and grab some lunch with you guys."

Jody followed her mother down the hatch.

"Brittany, are you on-line?" Gina asked.

"No," Brittany replied, turning from the computer.

"That's fine then; don't let me interrupt you," Gina said with a quick smile. "I was just checking because I want to send an e-mail."

Jody watched her mother sit down with her laptop. "Are you worried about Aunt Maria?" she guessed.

Gina nodded, her fingers flying over the keyboard. "She promised to keep me up to speed. But there's

Having a heart-to-heart with Mom

never an answer when I try to phone her. I thought if I sent her an e-mail and copied it to Mike, at least one of them would reply!"

Mike was Maria's husband. Jody nodded soberly, twiddling her silver dolphin.

Maddie came down the hatch a few minutes later. "Okay, Brittany," she said. "Let's see what you've done!"

111

As she spoke, she picked up the sheet lying on the table beside Brittany. She looked dismayed. "But you haven't answered any of the questions!"

"I'm sorry," said Brittany. But she didn't sound apologetic. "I got so interested in exploring this CD-ROM. . . ."

Maddie shook her head, gently reproving. "I know it's tempting to read on, but you have to learn to focus," she said. She sighed. "Well, you can probably still get it done before lunch."

Brittany frowned, then looked pleadingly. "Can't I do it later? Or do something else? I was reading about President John F. Kennedy and Martin Luther King."

"That wasn't the assignment, Brittany. Here," Maddie said firmly. She pushed the textbook on the table closer to Brittany. "Leave the computer now. Read chapter one and answer the questions. You have half an hour."

Brittany looked stubborn. "I'll do it later."

"You'll have other things to do later," Maddie told her. "Do this now."

They stared at each other. Maddie looked firm. Brittany's gaze was turning hostile.

"Come on, Britt, it won't take long," Jody said, trying to break the tension. "I'll help you."

Brittany turned on her. "I don't need your help! I guess you think it's too hard for me — well, it's not! I *can* do it — I just don't *want* to. And nobody can make me!"

"That's enough!" Gina's voice was like a whiplash. When Jody turned to look she saw that her mother's dark eyes were snapping, and she wore the expression that would have had her brothers running for cover.

"No more nonsense out of you, Brittany! Maddie is your teacher, and you have to do what she tells you, the same as if you were in school." Gina spoke as if it were settled. She obviously didn't expect any argument. She stood up, closing her laptop.

Brittany swallowed hard, looking unhappy. Jody was sure she would back down. But then she saw her glance at the question sheet on the table and her expression hardened.

Looking back at Gina, Brittany said flatly, "But this isn't a school, and Maddie isn't my teacher. And you're not even related to me, *Aunt Gina.* I don't have to do what you say."

"Think again." Gina's voice was soft and dangerous.

Jody shivered and wondered how long her mother would be able to keep her temper under control.

Gina went on, "If you want to stay aboard *Dolphin Dreamer,* then you have to follow the rules. That means obeying Maddie — and me." She waited.

Brittany lifted her chin. "And what if I won't?"

"Then you'll have to leave," Gina replied crisply. "Your father can send you away to boarding school, and you can throw your little tantrums there." She gave Brittany a steely look and said, very quietly, "It's your call, Brittany."

8

J ody waited for Brittany to back down and apologize.
She wouldn't have been surprised to see the other girl
burst into tears. She almost felt sorry for Brittany, having
Gina so angry with her, even though it was her own fault.

Brittany took a deep breath. Then she turned away
from Gina, from all of them, and headed for the door.

"Come back here," Gina said sharply.

Brittany didn't even slow down. "No!" she shouted,
without looking back. "You can send me away — I
know you want to. Well, I don't care! Do what you like!
I hate you all!"

A moment later, they heard the sound of a cabin door slamming.

"Well," Gina said quietly, "I guess that's that."

She sounded defeated, Jody thought, watching as her mother climbed out of the hatchway.

Maddie looked at Jody. "Where did *that* come from?" she asked in amazement.

Jody shrugged.

"She solved all those algebra problems," Maddie said thoughtfully. "She seemed interested when I was talking about Native American cultures. Why couldn't she answer a few simple questions?"

"She just didn't want to do it," Jody said. "She's spoiled — I guess her mother lets her get away with not doing things."

Maddie wasn't convinced. "No, I'm sure there's more to it. But if she won't tell us. . . ." She sighed and shook her head, brooding on the problem.

Jody shrugged awkwardly. "I'm going out to talk to Mom," she said.

To her surprise, Maddie said, "I'll come with you."

Gina was on deck talking to Harry. "I'm afraid there's

no alternative. If she won't let Maddie teach her, Brittany simply can't stay," she concluded.

Harry's rugged, bearded face sagged unhappily. "Of course," he said quietly. "But I don't understand. I thought she'd settled down. She's really taken to you, Gina, especially. . . ."

Gina gave a short, unamused laugh. "Well, I'm definitely not her favorite person right now!"

"Harry," Maddie said, "does Brittany usually have problems with school?"

He shook his head. "Not now, as far as I know. She had learning difficulties a few years ago, but she repeated the second grade and that seemed to sort things out."

That explained why Brittany was a year older but they were still in the same grade, thought Jody.

Maddie looked interested. "You kept her back a year? Why?"

"She wasn't learning to read," Harry explained. "But that was years ago. I'm sure there's no problem now. She can do the work. Her grades are well above average. I've seen her report cards."

"I wish I had," said Maddie. She shook her head, a rueful expression on her face. "Harry, would you do me a favor?"

"Certainly," he replied.

"Please ask Brittany's mother if she was getting any learning support at school, or if there's anything a new teacher should know," Maddie said.

Harry looked puzzled. He glanced at Gina. "But Brittany isn't going to be your problem anymore," he began.

"If you're sending her away, then it's important for you to know what to tell her new school," Maddie pointed out. "I'd really like to talk to her last school. . . ." She broke off with an apologetic look at Gina. "I mean, I would if *I* was going to be teaching her," she said.

Gina sighed. "To be honest, I'd rather not send her away," she said quietly. "I'm sure that being here with her father is better for Brittany than any boarding school. But she has to be willing to be part of the team — otherwise it won't work. If Brittany wants to stay, she'll have to apologize — and show she means it," Gina went on. "She can't change her mind in six months' time, when we're in the middle of the Pacific Ocean! If she can't accept the rules, she'd better go now."

Harry nodded. "I'll make a few phone calls," he said. He sighed. "I only want what's best for her," he said sadly.

Lunch was a subdued meal. Brittany did not appear, and no one mentioned her name. Mei Lin's Chinese chicken noodle salad was as delicious as always, but only Sean, Jimmy, and Dr. Taylor seemed to really appreciate it.

Afterward, Jody looked into their cabin. Brittany was lying on her bunk, facing the wall. Jody paused, then said, "Brittany? Want to talk?" She had no idea what she would say.

But Brittany didn't reply or even move. She might have been asleep.

Jody sighed and went back to join her mother and brothers, who were getting ready to go to Dolphin Haven.

As they were walking, Gina's cell phone began to

ring. She held it to her ear. "Hello . . . Mike! How's Maria? Where is she?"

Jody stared at her mother and saw her biting her lip nervously.

Gina caught her breath. "The hospital! Is she — you're sure she's all right? Really? Please tell me. Uh-huh. Uh-huh." She nodded several times and finally said, "Okay. Thank you for calling, Mike. Tell Maria to give me a ring sometime, okay? Bye."

"What's wrong?" Jody asked. "Was that Uncle Mike?"

Gina nodded. "Maria's in the hospital — they want to keep her in for a couple of days. He says there's nothing wrong, and that it's just a precaution."

Jody could tell that her mother didn't entirely believe this. She grabbed her mother's hand and squeezed it. "I'm sure she'll be fine. If something *is* wrong, they can look after her in the hospital. It's the best place for her to be." She tried to sound sure of herself.

Gina squeezed her hand back, sighed, and gave her a faint smile. "You're right, honey. Anyway, no sense in worrying. There's nothing I can do. We'll just have to wait and hope."

*   *   *

Jody's mood lifted when she reached the nursery pool. Misty came swimming right up to her and gave her calf a nudge to the surface. For the first time, Jody and the baby dolphin gazed at each other, face-to-face. With its big dark eyes the calf looked like a small replica of its mother.

Jody felt happiness bubbling up inside her. "Are you introducing me to your baby?" she asked Misty softly. "It sure looks like it! I think it's high time your baby had a name, don't you?"

Misty chattered and whistled.

Although she couldn't understand what Misty was saying, Jody thought the dolphin was trying to tell her something. "Do you mean you've already given him a name?" she asked.

Suddenly, she felt rather silly. "Of course, you wouldn't wait for somebody else to name him . . . and you wouldn't call him by a human name! But since we can't understand your dolphin language — not yet, anyway! — we have to give you names that people can say." She scratched her head thoughtfully. "I wonder, do you have dolphin names for your human friends? Do you have a name for me?"

But Misty did not reply. She'd noticed that her calf was straying. With a flick of her tail, she was off to round him up. Bella moved at the same time, cutting off his escape and pushing him gently back to his mother.

Jody watched the three dolphins swim away together toward the far end of the pool. The calf moved clumsily, thrashing its tail a lot. There was still a lot for him to learn before he would be able to move as gracefully as his mother.

Smiling to herself, Jody went up to the office, where she found her mother with Alicia and Tamika huddled around a computer. She paused in the doorway.

Gina looked up and smiled. "Come on in, honey," she said. "We're drafting an announcement about Misty's calf."

"Does he have a name yet?" Jody asked, going to join them. She looked at the picture of Misty and her baby on the screen.

"That's what this is all about," Alicia explained. "We're

asking for suggestions from anyone who's interested. Then Dan and I will choose the one we like best."

"You mean *I* might to get to name the baby?" Jody asked excitedly.

Alicia smiled and nodded. "If you give the best suggestion!"

"I'll try!" Jody promised. She wandered away, going over possibilities in her mind. She was glad to have something other than Brittany's latest explosion to occupy her mind. Trying to think up a name for Misty's baby was much more fun.

It was late when they finally left Dolphin Haven. Jody could hardly tear herself away from the dolphins in the nursery pool.

Gina admitted she felt the same. "If I could, I'd personally keep a twenty-four-hour watch on Evie," she said ruefully.

"So would I," Alicia agreed. "But it's not humanly possible! Remember, whether you're here or not, somebody will be watching over her — and we'll call you if anything happens," she promised as she waved good-bye to them.

Jody wasn't surprised to find Brittany asleep — although she did wonder if her cabin mate had spent the entire day in bed! She didn't stir when Jody came in and switched on a small light.

As she was getting undressed, Jody noticed a piece of paper lying out. It was the question sheet that Maddie had given them, and it seemed that Brittany had finally decided to fill in the answers.

As she glanced at it, Jody frowned. She wondered if Brittany had made a mess of it on purpose — or was her handwriting always that bad? Between the sloppy writing and the incredible number of spelling mistakes, Jody had no idea whether the answers were right or not.

There was the sound of a muffled sob.

"Brittany?" Jody asked cautiously.

The sobbing burst out uncontrollably.

Jody went and perched on the edge of Brittany's bunk. She listened to the sound of crying, feeling helpless. Then she put her hand on Brittany's covered shoulder.

Brittany rolled over to face her. "I don't want to go away," she wept. "I want to stay here! I know I said I hated you all, but I don't! I really like Aunt Gina and Maddie, but I was so horrible that now they must really hate *me*!"

Poor Britt

"No, they don't," Jody told her. "Mom got mad at you, but she doesn't hate you. She's really worried about you."

Brittany stopped crying. She blinked up at Jody, sniffling and shuddering. "She is?"

Jody nodded.

"Do you think your parents might let me stay? If I told them I'm really, really sorry?" Brittany asked haltingly.

Jody bit her lip. Then she nodded. "But you'll have to do more than just say you're sorry," she warned. "If you want to stay, you have to do what you're told. You can't keep throwing tantrums — and you won't get away with not doing schoolwork."

At this, Brittany's face crumpled. She began to cry again.

Jody sighed. She was tired, and she felt her patience wearing thin. "Oh, come on, Brittany, what's the big deal? Didn't you go to school in Florida? I thought you said you're in seventh grade. Look, just stop crying and tell me what's wrong!"

After a few seconds, Brittany got herself under control. "My work's over there. Go look at it."

Not wanting to admit she already had — Brittany would probably accuse her of spying — Jody went and picked up the sheet of paper. "Is your writing always this bad?" she asked.

"That took me *hours*," Brittany said flatly. "I know you won't believe me and neither will Maddie, but I did my best. My last school let me use a computer with a spell checker, and then I was okay. If I have to write by hand, I keep putting letters in the wrong order."

She sighed heavily. "But Maddie wouldn't let me use the computer. Just like at my first school — they said I just needed to try harder — when I was already trying as hard as I could! And I'll bet whatever school Daddy sends me to will think I'm doing it on purpose, and I'll get rotten grades, and everybody will hate me. . . ." She burst into tears again.

Jody thought about what she'd heard earlier in the day. "Listen to me, Brittany," she said urgently. "Maddie was asking your dad if you needed extra help — she said she'd really like to talk to someone at your last school."

Brittany sniffed hard, looking startled. She managed to croak out, "She did?"

Jody nodded. "She didn't think you were just being a spoiled brat . . . and Harry said you got good grades last year."

Brittany nodded vigorously, her tears drying up. "I did, too! The school had some special computer programs for me, and the teachers gave me extra time if I needed it. They didn't think I was stupid, or bad, or slow. They said they thought I was dyslexic — and that lots of very smart people are!"

"I bet Maddie would help you, too, if she knew," Jody said. "I know she wants to."

"Really?" Brittany stared at her hopefully. Then her face crumpled. "But your mom won't let me stay. I was so horrible to her. . . ." Her voice caught.

"Go and apologize to her," Jody said quickly. "Tell her what you just told me. And then tell Maddie. If you tell Mom how much you really want to stay, I'm sure she'll let you."

"You really think so?" Brittany wiped her eyes with her pajama sleeve.

Jody nodded and stood up. "Go on. The sooner you get it over with, the better."

Brittany looked apprehensive. "What, now? I don't know what to say. . . ."

"You could start with 'I'm sorry,'" Jody suggested.

Brittany nodded. "But — I can't go by myself!" she said. "I just can't face Aunt Gina. Not after I was so awful to her!"

Jody saw that Brittany really did look frightened. She smiled ruefully. "Honestly, it'll be okay! I promise! Mom's not going to eat you! Come on, then. We'll go together."

Gina and Craig were in the main cabin with Harry. They looked surprised to see the two girls.

"I thought you'd be asleep by now," said Gina.

Jody looked at Brittany. "Brittany couldn't sleep because there's something she wanted to say to you," she said.

They all looked at Brittany, who stood as if frozen, saying nothing.

Jody gave Brittany a little push, and that seemed to do the trick.

"I — I'm sorry I was so horrible to you before," Brittany began, gazing at Gina. "I won't do it again — I promise, I'll do whatever you tell me, if you let me stay. Please don't send me away!"

Gina looked at her searchingly. "Apology accepted," she said. "But Brittany, before I can believe you've changed your attitude, I need more than a promise. How do I know something else won't make you fly off the handle like that again? Can you explain it to me? Why wouldn't you do your assignment for Maddie?"

"I've done it now," Brittany said. "I couldn't do it before — I just couldn't, that's all!" For a moment, it seemed as if she was about to burst into tears.

Harry moved toward her but then checked himself, looking deeply unhappy.

Jody looked at her mother's disappointed face and knew Gina thought this was just more of Brittany's stubbornness. "Brittany's dyslexic," she said quietly.

There was a startled pause.

Then Brittany nodded. "I have to concentrate really hard to understand when I'm reading," she began. "And when I try to write, somehow it all comes out wrong. . . . It looks awful! And when Maddie said I had to write by hand, I knew it would take me forever, and it still wouldn't be right. . . . At my last school, they let me use a computer. They said I can't help it, and I *am* a hard worker!" Brittany stopped to draw breath, still looking as if she might burst into tears any second.

She looked at the floor, then added, "I didn't want Jody to see my scribbles. I didn't want her and Maddie to think I wasn't smart."

"You'd rather we all thought you were spoiled and uncooperative," Gina murmured, her mouth twisting wryly. "Oh, Brittany . . ."

"Sweetheart, I'm so sorry — I should have known!" Harry exclaimed, looking very upset. "It's my fault for not keeping in closer touch with you!"

Brittany turned to him. "Please don't send me away, Daddy! Let me stay!" She looked pleadingly at Gina. "I promise, I'll do whatever you, and Uncle Craig, and Maddie tell me!"

Harry turned to look at Gina, too, waiting anxiously for her answer.

Gina smiled and then said, "Brittany . . . after what you've just told us . . . honey, of course you can stay!"

9

August 28 — late afternoon — Dolphin Haven.

I'm sitting with my feet in the water of the nursery pool, trying to keep cool. The clouds are gathering, and the air is really still. A stormy sort of feeling. I guess it will rain soon. That would make the evening a little cooler. We've been invited to stay for dinner. Brittany is in the kitchen now, helping Maddie make a big salad.

Bella still hasn't given birth — even though everybody thought she would be the first. Surely it will happen by tonight? She looks the same as ever, though, swimming around with the others.

Misty's calf is still doing fine, gaining weight every day, and getting stronger and bolder. But his "aunts" always make sure he doesn't stray too far from his mom! No name yet, but Lindsay e-mailed me some great ideas. I told her I was trying to think of a name starting with "M" and she reminded me that I'd described his birth as "magical." So why not call him Magic? Or else name him after a famous magical figure, like Merlin?

Merlin and Magic are both great names. I couldn't decide which one I liked better, so I entered them both. I hope one of them wins. Then it would be almost like Lindsay was here, sharing everything with me. I really miss her. . . .

A rumble of thunder made Jody look up from her writing. She jumped up quickly and hurried toward the buildings, reaching their shelter just before the first, heavy raindrops thudded down.

The tropical thunderstorm was fierce while it lasted, but it had passed over by the time everyone was sitting down to dinner at Alicia and Dan's huge old kitchen table.

Jody looked around, checking them all off a mental

list: Mom, Dad, Maddie, Brittany, Dr. Taylor, Tamika, Alicia, Dan. The twins had decided to take a break from dolphins and go fishing with Cam instead. She frowned. "Who's keeping watch on the dolphins?" she asked.

"Rachel and Josh," Dan replied, setting down a huge pot of chili between the salad bowl and the bread basket on the table.

Jody sighed with relief. She'd nearly forgotten the two graduate students from Texas. They had arrived a few days earlier and had shown themselves to be utterly devoted — to each other and to studying dolphins.

"They'll have something to eat later," Alicia explained as she began to ladle out the chili and pass the bowls down the table.

"Mmm, that smells great," Craig said appreciatively. "I could eat a horse."

"Sorry, we don't do horsemeat in this kitchen," Alicia replied, making a face at him.

The telephone clipped to Dan's belt gave its warbling ring. Everyone went silent as they waited for him to answer.

"Dan *Levy*," he said crisply. "Rachel! What's up? Yes, that sounds like it — we'll be right out!"

Jody gave a yell of excitement. "Bella's having her baby!"

Alicia checked with Dan. "It *is* Bella?"

"Yep." He grinned, pushing back from the table. "The others are gathered around her in a way that sounds *very* familiar. I think we're about to have a new birth to celebrate!"

Dinner was forgotten as everyone hurried out to the poolside — although Jody heard Dr. Taylor give a sad little sigh and saw him grab a bread roll before leaving the table.

"Now everyone, please keep quiet," Dan said earnestly as they neared the poolside. The excited chatter died down at once. He smiled sympathetically. "Remember, even though Bella is an experienced mother and is used to having lots of people around, giving birth can be stressful. She needs peace and quiet and the support of her friends, which she has. However excited we feel, let's not distract her."

Everyone nodded in agreement. Gazing down into the clear water of the pool, Jody saw Bella give a faint shudder. Her body flexed and straightened and flexed again. Lola and Evie pressed close, one on either side of Bella. Jody was sure that their nearness was comforting to Bella and would help to give her the strength she needed.

After a few minutes, Evie slipped beneath Bella and pushed her up toward the surface to breathe. Bella rested there a moment, then, still partly supported by Evie, her body flexed again.

"I think this is it," Dan said, low-voiced.

Gina was watching everything through the eyepiece of the camcorder. Jody heard her gasp.

At the same time Brittany said, "I can see the head!"

Jody's stomach clenched with dread at these words. She knew dolphins were supposed to be born tailfirst. Surely Brittany was wrong. But as she leaned forward, straining to see what was happening, Jody glimpsed the calf's long, pointed snout emerging from Bella's body. And then she could see an eye, and the rounded melon of its head.

Alicia gave a low groan, and around the pool people were shifting position, murmuring uneasily.

Jody shivered, suddenly very frightened. She clutched the little silver dolphin she wore on a fine chain around her neck and wished as hard as she could for the baby's safety.

"It may be all right," Dan said quietly, like an answer to her wish. "Tailfirst is normal, but recent research suggests that headfirst births are a lot more common than we used to think."

Dan's words were encouraging, but the cheery mood had gone. Now everyone was worried.

The rest of the birth went very quickly. The calf slipped all the way out of its mother and wriggled in the water. Bella gave a sudden sharp twist of her body, snapping the umbilical cord.

Lola darted forward. Swimming beneath the newborn calf, she began to nudge and guide it toward the surface. It seemed to need more help than Misty's calf had. Making her signature whistle again and again, Bella joined her daughter in pushing the newborn to the surface.

"It's not moving," Gina said suddenly, her voice tense and worried.

"Yes, it is," said Brittany. "I can see it moving!"

Jody couldn't tell. The calf was certainly moving through the water, but was that just because Bella and Lola were pushing it along, or was it trying to swim as well? She held her breath in an agony of suspense as she watched.

"It's not breathing," said Alicia. Her voice broke into a little sob of worry.

Jody stared at the little dolphin, trying to will it to breathe.

Together, Lola and Bella held it pushed up above the water's surface. It didn't matter how weak the newborn calf was, the touch of the air should have triggered the breathing instinct, making it open its blowhole.

But the calf didn't move.

"I'm afraid we've lost it," said Dan quietly, putting his arm around Alicia. "Poor Bella."

Jody blinked hard. She shook her head angrily, fighting the tears and the lump in her throat. She refused to cry, because that would mean she'd given up.

Bella and Lola hadn't given up. They were still holding the calf to the surface, giving it a chance to live. Jody tore her eyes away from the sad little scene in the water and looked at Dan and Alicia, who were holding each other.

"Can't you do *something*?" she pleaded. "You're both vets! Can't you save Bella's calf?"

Dan shook his head. "The calf is past saving," he said quietly. "It's dead. I'm afraid it never really lived."

"But why?" Jody burst out. "What went wrong?"

Alicia answered. "We don't know. Bella did everything right. She was healthy. . . . We did everything we could for her . . . but . . ." She waved one hand helplessly. Her eyes were bright with tears. "A lot of newborn dolphins simply don't survive. We don't know why."

Jody had never felt so hopeless and miserable. She began to cry. The sobs were huge and wrenching, shaking her whole body.

It's not fair!

Then she felt someone hugging her. It took a moment for her to realize that it was Brittany.

August 28 — evening — Dolphin Haven.
Bella's baby is dead! The poor little calf never took its first breath. I can't stop crying. Poor, poor Bella.
Everybody else is having dinner now — Alicia reheated

the chili — but I just couldn't eat, so I volunteered to keep watch. I'm sitting alone in Alicia's office, keeping an eye on the closed-circuit TV.

Dan thought it best for everyone to keep away from the pool for a while, to let Bella and the others come to terms with what has happened.

Alicia reminded us all that we have to concentrate on Misty's calf and on Evie, who will soon be giving birth. I'm scared about that now. Before, I was so excited, but I can't bear to see another newborn dolphin die. If Bella's baby didn't make it, what chance does poor old Evie's have? Evie has never had a baby survive, and she is so old now that everybody thinks this is probably her last chance to be a mother.

The next day, over muffins and coffee in their kitchen, Dan and Alicia filled in everyone on the situation.

The mood in the crowded room was somber. Only Dr. Taylor and the twins showed any interest in the muffins.

"We haven't had a chance yet to run any tests on the dead calf," Dan said. "But we're guessing that the headfirst birth means that the calf wasn't able to receive enough oxygen through the umbilical cord. It was obviously very weak when it was born. Now that we've retrieved the body, we hope to learn more."

He took a deep breath and went on. "On a more positive note, I'd like to point out that Bella is still relatively young and healthy. She's given birth to healthy calves before and raised them successfully, and we have every reason to believe she'll do so again. It is even possible that by next year we'll be able to announce a new pregnancy."

Sean raised his hand.

Looking surprised, Dan nodded at him. "Um, is it Sean or Jimmy? You have a question?"

"I'm Sean. What I want to know is, how does Bella feel? Is she sad?"

Dan sighed. "We can't assume that dolphins experience things exactly as humans do," he said carefully. "We don't know exactly what she's feeling — we can only guess — and observe her behavior."

"Well, does she know that her baby is dead?" Brittany asked.

"Oh, yes," he said, nodding. "It was obvious she understood when she stopped giving her signature whistle and stopped trying to hold the calf up to the surface. But even then, when she'd given up, she stayed beside the body for the rest of the day."

"She didn't even respond to us at feeding time," Alicia put in.

"That's worrying," Gina said with a frown.

Alicia shook her head. "I think it's natural grieving behavior. And we didn't want to try to force her. We let her decide how long she needed to stay beside the body. She left it this morning and came to us to be fed."

"Bella's moved on," Dan concluded. "I think we should, too. We need to look to the future — right now, specifically, Evie's future."

10

September 10 — midafternoon.

We've been waiting days and days, but still no sign of Evie's baby. Everybody is getting tense, even though Dan says this is a good sign, as in the past she had miscarried before the calf was fully developed.

Brittany and I are getting along much better. Now that everybody knows her "deep, dark secret" it's no big deal. Maddie heard from Brittany's last school and found out more details about what sort of help she needs and what programs they were using. Right now, we are waiting for her to finish today's schoolwork so we can join the others

*at Dolphin Haven — okay, she's ready. Perhaps today will
be the day!*

When Jody, Brittany, Maddie, Sean, and Jimmy
arrived at Dolphin Haven, they immediately
noticed a lot of activity around the nursery pool.

Alicia was in the shallow water beside Evie, and
Tamika and Dan were both at the waterside, helping
her with something. Gina was filming, while Craig and
the visiting researchers looked on.

Jody's heart pounded with excitement and fear. Was
Evie having her baby? Had something gone wrong?
She broke into a run. "Why didn't you call us?" she de-
manded, rushing up to her mother.

"Take it easy, honey," said Craig.

Gina explained, "They're just giving Evie a scan, to
make sure everything is all right."

Now Jody saw that the equipment at the edge of the
pool was the ultrasound monitoring unit. Evie was lying still in the water as she had been trained to do,
while Alicia rolled the scanner gently but firmly along
her flank.

Dan gazed at the blurry gray image that appeared on the screen. He nodded, seeming pleased with what he saw, and told them, "It seems fine. I don't think it has much more growing room, though. I'd really expect Evie to give birth within the next forty-eight hours!"

A wave of excitement rippled through the watchers around the pool.

"Off you go, Evie, my girl," said Alicia, giving the big dolphin a friendly pat.

Jody watched Evie swim slowly away to join the others.

"How's Bella doing?" Maddie asked as Alicia got out of the pool.

"Much better," Alicia replied. "In fact, she's absolutely fine. She seems to be nearly as devoted to Merlin as Misty is herself! You couldn't ask for a pair of more helpful aunts than Bella and Lola!"

"Sometimes it gets a little out of hand," Dan said with a laugh. "They practically fall over each other to be the first to help . . . and of course, in a little pool like this, Misty doesn't really need that much help to look after one calf!"

"It'll be better when Evie's calf is born," Gina said. "Then there will be two babies for the baby-sitters to look after!"

Everyone laughed — but a little uneasily. Jody could tell that they were all thinking the same thing: Not long ago *three* calves had been expected. She clutched the little silver dolphin at her neck, frowning anxiously. Would Evie's baby be all right?

The McGraths, Maddie, and Brittany went back to *Dolphin Dreamer* for dinner, but they returned to Dolphin Haven afterward.

Though none of them was scheduled to keep watch on Evie that evening, no one wanted to miss anything. Jody suspected that everyone was hoping to be the first to notice that Evie's labor had started.

Even the twins had caught this "calf fever" (as Craig jokingly called it) and would crouch quietly beside the pool for minutes at a time, gazing intently into the water. Jody thought she had never seen them sit still for so long without doing anything.

When Gina said it was time to go back to the boat to

bed, Jody groaned, but her protest was halfhearted. She had seen Evie eat her fill at feeding time, and Dan had suggested she was still some way off from giving birth.

"Tomorrow we'll bring our sleeping bags," Craig promised. "And we won't leave until Evie's calf has been born!"

"Oh, boy, we're going to camp out!" Sean excitedly punched his brother on the arm. Jimmy began to jump around with glee.

Brittany and Jody exchanged a resigned glance, sighing in unison.

"Let's hope you don't have to," said Alicia. "Who knows? Maybe Evie will break the tradition and have her calf in the morning, after we've all had a good night's sleep!"

Brittany spoke up suddenly. "If Evie has her baby just after the sun comes up, you could call her Dawn!" she suggested.

"That would be a lovely name," Alicia agreed. She glanced at her husband, who smiled approvingly. She turned back to Brittany. "If that calf is female, we might go for the name Dawn no matter when she's born!"

Jody nodded enthusiastically, and Brittany glowed with pleasure.

They had just returned to *Dolphin Dreamer* and seen the twins stagger off to bed when Gina's cell phone began to ring.

Brittany gasped. "Evie!"

Jody watched her mother anxiously, ready to race back again if she gave the sign.

"Hello?" said Gina into the phone. Suddenly, she looked worried. "Maria! Are you all right?" Then she relaxed and smiled. "Oh, that's great. What did they say? That's wonderful! Oh, I'm so pleased! Thanks for calling. . . . No, Evie hasn't had her calf yet. We're hoping it'll be tomorrow. Yes, of course I'll let you know . . . I'll call you tomorrow, and we can have a good chat. Yeah. I will. Bye."

"Aunt Maria?" Jody asked when the call was finished. She could tell from her mother's face that the news was good.

Gina nodded, smiling. "The hospital sent her home. Her doctor is very pleased. Her blood pressure has gone down. And what's even better, they think that her pregnancy is no longer at risk!"

Jody rushed to hug her mother. She collided with her dad, who'd had the same idea, but they managed to sort it out, and all hugged one another, laughing.

When they pulled apart, Jody noticed Brittany looking slightly awkward and left out.

Gina noticed, too, and stretched out her arms. "Come on, Brittany, give your Aunt Gina a hug — it sounds like you're going to have another honorary cousin come spring!"

Brittany's tight expression melted into a shy smile, and she rushed into Gina's embrace.

"I'll make us a pot of tea," Craig suggested.

"Better make it chamomile, honey," Gina said. "We need to get some sleep."

"Yes, *lots* of honey in mine, please," Jody joked. She thought chamomile tea tasted like hay steeped in hot water.

"I remember," said Craig with a grin.

He hadn't even reached the galley when the cell phone began to ring again.

"Hello?" Gina said. Her expression became alert. "We're on our way!" Breaking the connection, she said, "Evie's started labor."

"Let's go!" Jody exclaimed.

"What about Maddie?" Brittany asked.

"Good thinking!" Craig exclaimed. "I hope she hasn't gone to bed yet. . . . Would you go knock on her door and find out?" Then he made a wry face. "And I suppose I'd better do the same for Dr. Taylor . . . but if he's asleep, I'm not going to try to wake him!"

Outside, the big full moon made it seem nearly as light as day. Jody was so excited she couldn't help breaking into a run. But every time she slowed to catch her breath she found herself remembering poor Bella's calf. Everyone had been just as excited then, and even more hopeful — and then it had all gone horribly wrong. Her stomach twisted with anxiety as she wondered what would happen this time.

Gina caught up to Jody and put an arm around her. She seemed to read her mind. "Come on, think positive!" she said. "Evie's come this far . . . and after all, the scan today showed that the calf is big and healthy!"

Jody nodded. Her mom was right. She broke into a run again.

When they reached Dolphin Haven they found everyone gathered around the nursery pool in a quiet group. There was tension in the air. Jody saw Dan's veterinary kit, and some other equipment had been placed at the poolside.

"What's happened?" Gina asked softly as they approached.

Tamika turned and smiled a greeting. She shook her head. "Nothing, yet," she said. "About twenty minutes ago Alicia noticed that the dolphins seemed restless. Normally, all the activity seems centered around Misty and Merlin, but now that's changed. Evie started swimming in short little bursts and then resting. Bella and Lola have been sticking close to Evie and completely ignoring Misty."

"What's Misty doing?" Maddie asked.

Tamika glanced at the pool. "She's just keeping Merlin out of the way. She's been very vocal, though. They all have."

The distinctive sounds of the dolphins — clicks, pops, squeaks, and whistles — seemed to be all around, soft but distinct in the quiet night air.

Jody felt a surge of excitement and couldn't help smiling at the familiar yet mysterious noise.

"They sounded much the same during the other two births," Craig commented.

Tamika nodded. "Yes. I can't help thinking they're keeping Evie's spirits up, you know, like, 'You can do it, girl!'"

"And, 'Don't forget your breathing exercises!'" Maddie added with a wide grin.

They all smiled at one another, sharing the excitement.

"Is it all right if we move a bit closer?" Gina asked, hoisting her video camera.

"Sure," Tamika agreed. "Alicia said you'd want to film." She looked at Brittany and Jody with a friendly grin. "And you know all about keeping quiet!" She looked around. "You didn't bring the twins?"

"They were already asleep," Gina explained.

"Just like Dr. Taylor!" Craig added.

"He can watch it on video later, from a nice, comfy chair," said Gina, moving away to find a position with a good, clear view.

Jody hurried after her mother, with Brittany close behind.

Reaching the poolside, Jody stopped and gazed down. Moonlight sparkled on the water. She saw Evie's dark bulk resting not far below the surface. As she watched she saw her rise. Her blowhole made a little puffing sound as she took a breath of air before sinking again.

Bella and Lola were on either side of Evie. Jody could hear low, steady clicking sounds, muffled by the water. She saw Evie give a convulsive shudder. Her tail flexed. Then it flexed again.

Jody gasped as she saw something dark begin to emerge from beneath Evie's tail. She bent down, trying to make it out. Her hands were clenched into fists as she hoped for the best . . . and then she relaxed and heard her mother sigh behind her as they both saw that, yes, it was the calf's tail coming out!

Evie shuddered again. Bella slipped beneath her big, laboring body, pushing her up toward the surface and supporting her so that she could breathe.

Jody saw the smaller tail wriggle. Evie wriggled, too. Seconds later, the whole calf slipped out of Evie's body. Although small beside its mother, it was large for a baby. Jody could see that it was much bigger than Merlin had been at birth — probably even bigger than Merlin was now! She noticed that it had odd wrinkles on its face.

As if reading her mind, her mother murmured, "Those will smooth out in a day or two."

Around the pool, the watchers gave a collective sigh at the sight of the newborn.

But Jody still felt anxious. She knew the danger had not passed. She gazed at Evie, who seemed exhausted by this last effort and did not move. Nor did the calf, which floated in the water, still attached to its mother by an umbilical cord. Jody gnawed her lip, wondering why Bella didn't bite through it, as she had done for Misty.

Bella seemed to be waiting, though. After a moment,

Evie roused herself. The great body gave a sharp half turn, and she snapped the umbilicus herself, like an old pro.

"Oh, well done, Evie!" Alicia breathed.

As soon as Evie had separated herself from her newborn calf, Bella went into action. With Lola by her side she glided forward. Working together, Bella and Lola guided the calf to the surface. As soon as the top of the newborn's head cleared the water, the blowhole opened. Instinct took over; the baby gulped in its first breath of air before sinking back into the water.

But then it didn't seem to know what to do. It flailed around, tail and flippers pounding clumsily.

Bella came to the rescue, guiding the calf with her body, pushing and nudging it back to the safety of its mother.

As it bumped into Evie's big, solid body, the calf grew calmer. Bella kept on nudging it, guiding it, until it found the right spot beneath Evie's tail. There it latched on and began to suckle.

Jody felt her eyes sting with happy tears. Evie's calf had been born, and it was alive.

Bella and Lola take charge!

"A big, strong, healthy calf," Dan said quietly. "Well done, Evie."

"Well done, all the staff at Dolphin Haven," Craig put in. "Something tells me Evie wouldn't have managed without you."

"And Bella," Jody said. "Evie couldn't have managed without her aunts to help her." She fingered the silver dolphin at her neck as she spoke and gazed up at the night sky. The stars were like brilliant jewels against a cloth of black velvet. They looked like tiny diamonds, specks of light, but she knew that really they were huge suns shining far, far away. Did they shine down on other planets filled with life out there, or was Earth the only one?

Evie began to whistle the same distinctive notes over and over again. It was her signature whistle. She was telling her baby who she was. Everyone fell silent, listening to the song of the new mother dolphin.

You will find lots more about dolphins on these websites:

The Whale and Dolphin Conservation Society
www.wdcs.org

International Dolphin Watch
www.idw.org

Dolphin Diaries™

Look for Dolphin Diaries #5

CHASING THE DREAM

Over lunch, Jody asked Luisa to tell them more about the mysterious Frida.

"I don't believe it!" Brittany said loudly, before Luisa could reply. "Honestly, Jody, were you asleep, or did you flunk out of your first year of Spanish? Luisa told us all about Frida this morning!"

"Well, maybe the other people at this table would like to hear about her," Jody shot back, thinking quickly. But she could feel herself flushing.

"Who's Frida?" Gina asked, seeing an argument brewing.

"My best friend," Luisa said solemnly. Then her eyes crinkled as she smiled warmly and confessed, "I'm afraid I was teasing the girls a little. Actually, Frida is a dolphin who lives in the waters I patrol. She's a very special dolphin, and I know you are all going to want to meet her."

Jody's eyes widened in surprise.

"I never met a dolphin I didn't like," Craig said with a grin, as he helped himself to salad. "But what's so special about this Frida?"

"She's a hybrid," Luisa replied. "A cross between a bottle-nosed and an Atlantic spotted dolphin!"

Craig gave a low whistle. "I'd heard that such cross-breeds were possible, but I've never seen one."

"That *is* something, all right," Gina said. "I certainly do want to meet her!"

"Me, too!" Jody said excitedly. She piled salad onto her own plate and passed the bowl. "How did you find her?" she asked Luisa. "And how did you know what kind she was?"

"I first saw her about a year ago, when I came to live on *Amigo del Mar*," Luisa replied, smiling.

"That means 'Friend of the Sea,'" Brittany informed Jody with a superior smile.

"I know that!" Jody snapped. She caught her mother's disapproving look, but she couldn't help herself. Brittany had found one area where she was better than Jody, and she sure was making the most of it!

Luisa ignored their bickering. "The dolphin came up to me while I was swimming one day," she explained. "I was very surprised! I didn't try to approach her or touch her — WDPL advises never to do that — but Frida kept coming back. She seemed very curious about me, and she soon made it clear that she wanted to be friends. She was a solitary dolphin — I never saw her with a group — and she enjoyed my company. This sort of thing happens from time to time, you know, solitary dolphins making friends with people, but usually the *solitarios* are male."

"I'd like to hear more about your work, Luisa," said Maddie. "Isn't Mexico *the* major dealer in dolphins for the display industry throughout Latin America?"

"That is true, I'm sorry to say," Luisa replied sadly. "Not only does my country keep more dolphins in captivity than any other single nation — often in dreadful conditions — but it also acts as a sort of 'middleman' by allowing dolphins captured in the wild to be sold out of Mexico."

"Why?" Jody asked, her food forgotten as she listened.

Luisa turned to her. "Well, you see, some countries have much tighter regulations than others about trading in dolphins," she explained. "Many simply don't allow any dolphins to be imported, whether they were caught in the wild or born in captivity. But sadly, other countries are all too willing to buy dolphins from places like Mexico without asking too many questions about their origin."

"But that's wrong!" Jody exclaimed.

Luisa nodded her agreement. "Yes, of course it is. The laws in Mexico about importing and exporting dolphins must be changed. But that won't happen until enough people understand that capturing wild dolphins is a cruel business that must be stopped."

"So why aren't *you* in Mexico?" Brittany asked.

Jody winced. Brittany's blunt question sounded

rude. But Jody had been wondering the very same thing.

Brittany flushed slightly, looking embarrassed. "I'm sorry . . . I'm not criticizing . . ." she added quickly. "It's just that you sound so passionate about it, and, after all, it is your country, so I thought you'd want to be there, trying to change the laws."

Luisa smiled at Brittany. "That's okay. It's a good question. I have worked in Mexico, and I will again. And I am trying to change things there, wherever I can. I write letters to people who matter. And I write and translate articles for Mexican newspapers and magazines. Sometimes I get letters from people saying that something I've written has changed their minds, or they've joined an animal welfare organization because of my words. That makes me feel good. But when I started work for the Whale and Dolphin Protection League, I agreed to go wherever they sent me. And for now, that's Jamaica. The waters around nearby Cuba are a notorious capture location."

"What does that mean?" Sean asked, frowning. "Who gets captured?"

"Pirates?" Jimmy suggested, his freckled face hopeful.

Luisa laughed and shook her head. "I'm talking about dolphins," she reminded the boys. "A lot of dolphins are captured in the sea around Cuba and then exported all over the world."

"And you're there to stop them?" Sean asked eagerly.

"Like a policeman?" said Jimmy. "Do you get to arrest the dolphin thieves?"

Luisa's smile was wistful. "I wish! Unfortunately, it's not that simple." She sighed, her shoulders drooping. "The reason so many dolphins are taken from those waters is that it's very easy to get dolphin capture permits from Cuba. So alas, it's perfectly legal," she said.

"But it's wrong!" Jody said fiercely. She'd lost her appetite altogether, now.

"But surely there's something you can do," Craig said, frowning. "Otherwise, why would the WDPL bother to station a boat there?"

"I'm there to monitor the captures, so we stay informed about how many dolphins are being taken from the area. That's not information the Cuban government necessarily wants to give out, you see," Luisa explained. "Also, I'm conducting a population study to get some idea of the size of the dolphin population in those waters."

Jody noticed that Dr. Taylor seemed to perk up and take an interest when Luisa mentioned the population study. He looked like he wanted to ask a question, but his mouth was full. By the time he'd finished chewing, the conversation had moved on.

After he'd finished eating, Craig went up to take over the helm from Harry.

"Hey, Dad — can Sean and I help you sail?" Jimmy asked.

"Sure, if you've finished eating, come on!" Craig called back.

The two boys went scrambling after him.

A few moments later, Harry came down the hatch and took a place at the table.

"Here, let me give you some salad," Luisa offered.

"Thanks," the captain replied gruffly.

"How much longer do we have to sail?" Luisa asked.

Harry shrugged. "We should reach the northeast

coast of Jamaica by tomorrow," he told her. "Or the next day . . . Why don't you radio to your boat and get the precise coordinates? Then I can give you a better estimate."

"What a good idea!" Luisa exclaimed. "Do you mind if I do that now? Or later . . . I don't want to interrupt your lunch," she added apologetically.

Harry glanced across at Jody and Brittany, then turned back to Luisa. "One of the girls can show you to the control room," he said.

"I'm done," Jody said quickly, standing up. "I'll show you."

"Thanks, Jody," Luisa replied, getting up, too. She followed her to the small, forward cabin where the radio, charts, and navigational equipment were kept. She nodded at the sight of the radio. "Yes, it's just like mine — I understand how to use it."

Although Luisa didn't need her help, Jody hovered curiously. She heard Luisa make contact with a man called Frank. She knew that Frank also worked for the WDPL; he'd taken Luisa's place while she was away.

After Luisa had taken the coordinates, jotting them

on the palm of her hand with a pen, she said, "How are things there?"

"Not good." The man's voice sounded grim.

Luisa caught her breath. "What's been happening?"

The reply came: "A capture boat took four dolphins yesterday."

"Oh, no," Luisa groaned. Then she asked urgently, "What about Frida?"

"I don't know," said the man. "I was too far away to see anything except to count four dolphins taken. All I know is that I haven't seen any sign of Frida since yesterday morning. I haven't seen her since the capture boat left."

"Oh, Frank, no!" Luisa cried. Her face had gone pale, and she clenched her fists tightly.

The radio crackled, then the signal cleared. The voice came again. "I'm sorry, Luisa . . ."